SORORITY SUBTERFUGE

SHIELDMAIDEN SQUADRON: BOOK TWO

S.T. BENDE

Sorority Subterfuge
Shieldmaiden Squadron: Book Two
Copyright © 2021, S.T. Bende
Edited by: CREATING ink
Cover Art by: Melissa Stevens of The Illustrated Author Design
Services
ISBN: 978-1-950238-18-7

First publication: 2021, S.T. Bende

This book is a work of fiction. Names, characters, places, and
incidents either are products of the author's imagination or are used
fictitiously. Any resemblance to actual persons, living or dead,
events, or locales is entirely coincidental.

To my favorite little Vikings.

Meet the demigods in NIGHT WAR SAGA.

PROTECTOR

DEFENDER

REDEEMER

And introduce your Padawans to S.T.'s books for young readers!

Complete list of licensed children's titles at

www.stbende.com/kids-books/

CHAPTER 1

SORORITY GIRLS TALKED A lot.

Not all of them, obviously. And certainly not the one beside me, edging her way across the foyer and toward the front door. Poor Morgan reached for the handle, her fingers twitching as our sorority president chirped excitedly about our upcoming beach party with the neighboring fraternity. While Kayla bubbled on, Morgan's eyes grew wide with worry. She bore the telltale anxious look of a type-A student about to be late to class.

"So, anyway, it looks like we're all set for the Santa Monica Pier this weekend." Kayla flipped her glossy, black hair over one bare shoulder. "The Alphas will pick us up on Saturday at three. That should put us ahead of the Saturday night clubbing traffic, though of course the freeways in Los Angeles are *always* a nightmare. I mean, honestly, you'd think they'd have fixed things by now. They've been working on the 405 for-freaking-ever, am I right? My mom told me it was under construction when *she* went to So Cal State! But, whatever. Namaste, as my sister always says. Speaking of Kenzi, I need to see if she's still using my pink sweater or if I can have it back. I want to wear it on my date with Mike tonight because he *loves* when I'm in—"

"Um, Kayla?" Morgan hemmed. "Do you need me, or can I go to geology class?"

"Right. Sorry! I just wanted to make sure you'd double-checked on our insurance waivers. Everyone signed the November liability forms for off-campus travel, right?"

"We're all set," Morgan confirmed. "I collected the last ones at Monday night dinner. And I'd love to keep talking, but class starts in ten minutes and it's going to look *really* bad if all four of us walk in late."

Kayla's glossy, pink lips formed a pert *O*. Her amber eyes darted from me to my friends Janna and Brigga before settling back on Morgan. "Oh my god, I am so sorry. I totally forgot you guys had class. Nobody takes them this early. Morgan, you work in the scheduling office. Why don't you—"

"Kayla. There you are." Kayla's sister, Kenzi, padded barefoot across the wooden floor. She was still in the leggings and sports bra she'd worn to our six a.m. yoga class, but she'd added a flowy caftan and an armful of bracelets to her sporty ensemble. The beads clicked against her wrist as she raised her phone toward her sister. "Mom called. She wants to know if you want to join us for that meditation retreat over winter break."

"Erm . . . well, the thing is . . . I . . ." Kayla stared at her hot-pink fingernails.

Kenzi shot Morgan a wink. "*Go,*" she mouthed.

"Thank you," Morgan whispered. She opened the door and darted onto the porch. Janna, Brigga, and I slipped out behind her. When she'd cleared the steps, she turned to us with a furrowed brow. "We're going to have to book it if we want to make it to class on time. Professor Geryn hates it when people are late."

"I've always enjoyed a brisk morning run. Janna?" I adjusted my backpack and quickened my pace.

Beside me, my captain broke into a jog. "There's nothing like a sprint to get your blood flowing."

"A sprint . . ." Brigga matched our pace. "Or *that.*"

I followed her not-so-subtle finger as she pointed it up the street. Two shirtless men jogged our way. Sweat lined their muscled chests, the tiny droplets sliding over the ridges of their clearly defined abdomens. As they drew closer, I shifted my eyes reluctantly upward. Warmth filled my cheeks as I registered the signature smirk of Axel Andersson—my onetime trainer, and newly minted boyfriend.

Great Odin, is that what he looks like without his shirt?

"*Hei.*" Axel's running partner lifted one hand in greeting.

"Hi, Raynor," Brigga replied breathlessly.

"Ladies." Axel slowed to a stop. My friends and I did the same.

3

"Hey, Axel. Raynor." Morgan nodded. "We're just heading to class, so—"

"Morning, Ingrid." Axel leaned in to kiss my cheek. A surge of heat shot up my neck. As he pulled away, I caught a whiff of pine and sweat—the intoxicating blend that was so distinctly Axel. Nothing ever fazed him—not brutal Viking raiders, or angry reanimated dragons, or even the psychotic dark mage we'd traveled one thousand years into the future to destroy. When Axel was a teenager, his parents had left on a voyage and never returned. But instead of breaking down, Axel had kept calm and carried on, taking his place alongside the ruling family of Valkyris with seeming ease and grace. He was definitely inner-peace life goals.

Not that I'd ever tell him that.

Like Janna, Brigga, and I, Axel and Raynor weren't from around here . . . or now. The five of us were Viking-era warriors from the progressive clan of Valkyris. Under normal circumstances, we lived on an island in western Norway—one enchanted by *älva* dust and guided by the values of virtue, honor, and self-empowerment. But when a dark mage threatened our home, our chieftains sent us forward in time to capture him before he wreaked havoc on *this* world . . . and wiped ours clear out of existence. Since the locals had mistaken us for exchange students, we now lived in the Kappa Mu sorority house . . . where we were required to attend exchanges (sorority speak for exclusive parties), philanthropies (charity work), and of course, classes.

Classes we weren't supposed to be late for.

"We *really* have to go," Morgan called from halfway down the block. While I'd been zoning out on Axel's naked chest, she'd continued on her own mission: school or bust.

Right.

"See you at the gym?" I met my boyfriend's emerald eyes. "We should be done by eleven—eleven-fifteen if we have questions after the lecture."

"I'll see you there." Axel moved closer to whisper in my ear. "Hope you put up a better fight than you did last time. That was a pretty lousy show, Shieldmaiden."

My eyes narrowed. "Get ready to have your butt handed to you, Andersson."

Axel pulled away. He shot me a wink before jogging backward along the sidewalk. "Dream on."

My pulse spiked as he turned and sprinted toward the Alpha house. The muscles of his back flexed with each stride.

Gods, he was arrogant.

But look at his butt . . .

"Ingrid? You all right?"

"Um . . . yeah. I was just, uh . . ." I tore my gaze away from Axel's backside. My cheeks heated anew as I caught Janna's bemused stare.

"I think we all know what you were doing." Raynor chuckled as he jogged after his friend. "Later, Brigga."

"Bye!" Brigga waved.

Janna's eyes twinkled. "We'd better move. Morgan's going to have a heart attack."

"I'll just meet you guys there!" Morgan shouted. "No worries!"

"Poor Morgan." Brigga shook her head. "I can't believe you're making her late, Ingrid."

"Me? You were talking to Ray—"

"I'm kidding." Brigga laughed. "It was Kayla's fault, anyway. Come on. We can still get there on time if we run."

Brigga broke into a sprint. With one last look at Axel's retreating form, I tossed my crimson braid over my shoulder and took off after her. Geology didn't start for another five minutes. It would be tight, but we could definitely make it.

After all, shieldmaidens never backed down from a challenge.

By the time I reached the classroom, Morgan was doubled over just inside the door.

"Thank. God." She panted. "We. Made. It."

"You okay?" I patted her back.

"Yeah. I'm just not used to"—*Pant. Pant*—"impromptu sprints. Okay. Lecture time." She drew her shoulder blades together and inched her way along the row of students, her face flushed and her eyes to the ground. We claimed empty seats in the geology lecture hall just as Professor Geryn took his place at the podium.

Morgan breathed a heavy sigh of relief.

"Good morning, everyone. Shall we begin?" The middle-aged man with a receding hairline slid his glasses over his nose. He activated the smart screen behind him before looking up with a kind smile. "Today's lecture will be on the feldspar grouping of minerals—a collection that makes up more than forty percent of our planet's crust. Now, as you know, feldspar crystallizes from magma. It's frequently found in the sedimentary rocks so many of you are fond of bringing home from your hikes. Thank you, Britney, for the lovely sample you retrieved for me from your trip to San Diego last week."

"Of course!" a girl in the front row chirped.

"Before we get into the chemical composition of this group, I'd like to go over some of its practical applications. Let's see who's done the reading. Can anyone give me a common use for feldspar?" Professor Geryn scanned the sea of students. "Yes, Kafir?"

I hurriedly extracted a notebook from my bag as the boy three rows below lowered his hand. "Feldspar is a raw material utilized in ceramics and glassmaking."

"Very good," the professor praised. "Jules?"

"It's also used as a filler for rubber, plastics, and paint," a brunette in the back declared.

"Correct. Now, what about some scientific applications?" Professor Geryn's gaze moved around the room. My stomach dropped to my feet as his gaze roamed my row.

Please don't call on me. Please don't call on me. I'd been so consumed with tracking our dark mage, I hadn't bothered to crack open this textbook. Morgan called Geology "Rocks for Jocks," and had claimed it was so easy that *anyone* could pass it.

But the scientific applications of rocks weren't covered in shieldmaiden class.

Thankfully, Professor Geryn's attention shifted when my neighbor shot her hand into the air. "Yes, Morgan?"

"Feldspar is useful in multiple dating techniques, including argon-argon dating, potassium-argon dating, and luminescence-dating," she said. "And it's even been confirmed to exist on Mars, as noted in a report from the Curiosity Rover."

"Excellent." Professor Geryn changed the screen behind him.

My relief expelled in one slow exhale. "Thanks, Morgan."

She looked up from her notebook with a smile. "What are friends for?"

Exactly.

"Now, today we know the chemical composition of our main feldspars—aluminum, silicon, and oxygen combined with potassium, sodium, or calcium, most commonly. But our less scientific ancestors believed one of the sodium potassium aluminum silicates to be derived from the rays of the moon. Its formal name is hecatolite, but of course this *stone* is more commonly known as . . ." Professor Geryn held out his hands.

"Moonstone," chimed someone in the front half of the class. And Morgan.

"Moonstone," I muttered under my breath. Because I totally knew that.

Did not.

Wait . . .

"Moonstone." Brigga leaned over Janna. "Isn't that one of the—"

"Shh," I hissed. But I nodded—the name landed with me, too.

In pursuing our target, we'd discovered the dark mage had launched himself into the future to collect the ingredients for a spell—one that would give him complete control of Earth and enable him to wipe Valkyris from existence. We'd hoped the stone was something that was difficult to track—so maybe we could capture him *before* he managed to destroy our world.

But our teacher just said it made up forty percent of the planet?

"Now, moonstone is commonly found in Australia, Austria, Mexico, Norway, and right here in the states. It's frequently used in jewelry—in fact, it was crafted into key pieces of Greek and Roman ritual artifacts. After all, both cultures revered their moon deities. As did many others."

"Is he talking about Máni?" I whispered to Janna. The Norse moon god and his sun god brother, Sól, were a pretty big deal with our seers back home. The prophets performed monthly rituals that I'd never quite understood—bounty offerings, midnight trance dances, the whole deal.

I much preferred an early bedtime and a sunrise workout.

"Maybe," Janna whispered back.

"Several of these artifacts will be on display in two weeks' time at the geological museum right here on campus." Professor Geryn raised his chin. "Yours truly played a key role in curating this particular exhibit, and yes, extra credit *will* be awarded to those who both attend *and* write a five-page paper on the artifact of your choosing."

"Extra credit?" Morgan raised her voice. "Which artifacts will be there?"

"Far too many to name." Professor Geryn's eyes lit up. "But since you asked, my *personal* favorites are the Diadem of Latin Luna, the Scepter of Selene, and of course, the Orb of Máni. That last one is a particularly exquisite sample—it was discovered roughly one thousand years ago in western Norway, and it weighs in at more than twenty pounds. It's one of the most well-preserved pieces of moonstone ever found."

Goose bumps broke out across my forearms. *I knew it!*

"That's the piece." I leaned closer to Janna and Brigga. "That's what our dark mage is going after next."

Brigga flipped a page in her notebook. She tapped her pencil to the list she'd written on the parchment. At the top it read, *Spell to Control Mankind and All The*

Realms—the name of the mage's intended enchantment. Below, Brigga had listed the ingredients. She'd crossed off those he'd already collected.

"He's got the meteor rock and illy flower," Brigga said quietly. "But so far as we know he still needs quanta crystal—whatever that is—balboa bark, and a moonstone."

"And what better moonstone to collect than one belonging to Máni." I groaned. "Or any of the other *exquisite samples* that will be showing up right where we happen to be."

"We have to keep the target away from that exhibit," Janna whispered.

"Or . . ." My lips tugged upward.

Janna tilted her head. "What are you thinking?"

"I'm thinking that we don't know how to find him, and the best-preserved sample of one of his three remaining ingredients is going to be *right here on campus . . .*"

Brigga's brow quirked. "We know where he'll be."

"We don't know when he'll make a move for the specimen, but it's definitely going to happen," I confirmed. "Which means we can set up a sentry schedule, and—"

"Shh!" Morgan hissed from my right. "Professor Geryn's explaining the lab."

"Sorry, Morgan," I whispered. I turned to Janna and Brigga and mouthed, *"Talk later?"* They both nodded before returning their attention to the podium.

I shifted my shoulders and feigned focus. But I barely heard a word of the professor's instructions. For the first time in two weeks, we had a solid lead . . . and a real shot at taking down our target. We were back in the game.

Now all we had to do was win it.

CHAPTER 2

"*HEI*, SHIELDMAIDEN. YOU'RE LOOKING . . ." Axel's eyes moved slowly over my body before settling on the exposed section of skin at my midriff.

"Careful, Andersson," I warned.

"I was going to say fierce," he said defensively. "You're looking particularly fierce today."

"I look fierce every day." I crossed my arms over my chest.

Even I was distracted by this absurd training attire. But leggings and a "sports bra" were the preferred gym outfit for females at Southern California State. And I was nothing if not committed to this mission.

"My eyes are up here, Andersson." I tapped his forehead. The skin above his beard turned a light shade of pink. *Snort.*

"Right." Axel raked his fingers through the silky brown waves that fell around his shoulders. "I was just, uh . . ."

"Getting the weapons?" I dropped to a mat and reached for my toes. "What are we sparring with today? Short swords? Daggers?"

"Sticks." Axel tied his hair in bun. The muscles of his bare arms flexed with the movement.

Gods, he had spectacular arms.

"And my eyes are up here, Shieldmaiden."

"Shut up. Wait, sticks? What about the blades?"

"They installed a metal detector at the gym entrance." Axel shrugged. "I can't sneak the good stuff in anymore."

"Huh. That makes training more difficult." I bent one leg behind me and leaned over the other.

"We'll just have to find another place for blade training. The residences are out, but maybe we can locate an open space somewhere off campus. One of those hiking trails in the hills maybe, or the beach. We'll figure something out." Axel crossed to the corner of the room and pulled two thick wooden dowels from the wall. He tossed one onto the ground in front of me and held the other in his right hand. "They use these for something called *barre class*, but they'll suit our purposes well enough."

"If you say so." I swapped legs and stretched the other one. "Door's locked, right?"

Axel crossed to the doorway and jiggled the handle. He'd secured us one of the gym's small workout rooms —one at the back of the building. It lacked the weapons stash of our training rings back home, but it was the only private space we could find. And privacy was key for time-traveling Vikings on an undercover mission.

"*Ja*, it's locked," he confirmed. "Now, if you're finished stretching, can we get started already?"

"Impatient today?" I raised one arm above my head and gently pulled on my elbow.

"I've just been waiting around for you to show." Axel twirled his stick with one hand. "I warmed up twenty minutes ago."

"Sorry about that." I switched arms, tugging lightly on my left tricep. "We had to talk to our professor about the exhibit he's curating."

"What's he curing?"

"Cur-*ating*," I corrected. I quickly filled him in on the moonstones, Máni's orb, and the likelihood that our dark mage would be back on site in the next few weeks.

"So, you're saying we have another shot at trapping our target?" Axel moved into a two-handed spin. "Nice."

"It's more than nice." I picked up my own stick and pushed myself to my feet. "It could be our endgame. We catch him now, we can bring him home to Freia and Halvar before he gets any farther. Nobody hurts Valkyris. We continue to exist. We get out of here before *somebody* blows our cover . . ."

"Don't look at me." Axel dropped into a fighting pose. "I have more than adapted to twenty-first century college life."

"No kidding," I muttered. "You don't have to flirt with *every* girl who throws herself at you. I saw you walking those blondes back to their house last night."

"I can't help it if the Deltas have a thing for Norsemen." Axel tapped his stick lightly against mine. "Besides, you know I prefer redheads."

"Mmm-hmm." I leaned on my right leg and held my weapon parallel to the ground. Then I lunged forward. I brought my stick onto Axel's and swatted it down.

"Aw, don't be like that." Axel picked up his dowel and resumed his stance. "Nothing happened."

"I never said it did." I struck a second time, felling Axel's stick again.

"Why, Ingrid Tirsdatter." Axel retrieved his fallen weapon. He leapt forward, striking my stick with a force that left my hands vibrating. "If I didn't know better, I'd say you were jealous."

"Of some dim-witted Deltas?" I hit back, forcing Axel to duck. "I hardly think so."

"If it looks like a reindeer and walks like a reindeer . . ." Axel swung overhead. I wove to my right.

"Please." I drove low, and Axel tucked his knees to his chest. "If that's what you're into, then clearly I over-estimated the number of brain cells you have left in that thick, warrior head of yours."

"Thick, *Airborne Assassin* head," Axel corrected. He quick-stepped forward, alternating slices to either shoulder so that I was forced to retreat. "I'm captain of the *Airborne Assassins*. Warriors can't fly dragons. Have I taught you nothing?"

"Ah, there it is." I rolled to my right before leaping to my feet and striking Axel in the back. "The old Axel ego."

"Ouch." He spun around and jabbed at my stomach. I jumped backward, narrowly avoiding his attack.

"My words hurt? *Assassin?*" I swung in a low arc. Axel let out a groan as I connected with his calf.

"No." He batted my weapon to the ground with a swift strike. "But your stick did. You've got more force since we changed our training routine."

"The weights help." I scrambled backward, picking up my dowel and deflecting Axel's blow. "But I still prefer our boulder throws back home."

"Who doesn't?" Axel came at me again, but I parried each of his attacks before executing a sequence Janna and I had perfected at the shieldmaiden compound. I shuffled forward as I struck alternating blows to either side of his rib cage. Axel deflected admirably, rotating his hands in a quick series of parries. But I shifted my strategy just as he fell into a rhythm. With a fierce grunt, I drove my knuckles forward to deliver a swift punch to his gut. He exhaled heavily; the wind momentarily knocked out of him. As he sucked in a breath, I angled my fists upward and drove his hands higher. He pushed back. My heels dug into the ground as I launched us toward the edge of the room. Axel quickly stepped backward, but I matched his pace, driving forward and closing the distance between Axel and the wall. I kept the pressure on his forearms until they slammed against the padded surface. When I'd pinned them over his head, I pressed my stick firmly to his wrists, pushing against the pulse points as I drove my knee into his thigh.

Axel winced. With a groan, he opened his palms. His weapon fell to the ground. "You win."

"Obviously." I lowered my knee, but didn't let up the pressure on his arms.

"You're getting better," he panted.

"And you're getting worse." I raised my shoulder to my cheek, and wiped an errant trickle of sweat on the strap of my not-a-shirt. "Or are you going easy on me?"

"I would never," Axel vowed. "That wouldn't serve either of us. Or Valkyris."

"Valkyris." With a sigh, I transferred my stick to one hand and let my arms drop to my sides. Gods, I missed our home. The rolling greens. The Cliffs of Conquest. Helheim, I even missed those nightmare dragons Axel was so fond of flying. The Airborne Assassins' transports lived in the Dragehus—Valkyris' big, beachside barn. "Do you think we'll go home anytime soon?"

"We will." Axel reached out to tuck a loose curl behind my ear. "At some point in the next two weeks, we'll apprehend our target at the moonstone exhibit. We'll bring him back to Freia and Halvar, and life as we know it will return to normal."

"Easy as that, huh?" I leaned into the fingertip he ran along my cheek.

"Ja," Axel confirmed. He lowered his lips to my ear and exhaled gently. A wave of goose bumps broke out along my neck, and I inched a step closer.

"Good."

"Now," he whispered. "I'm well aware that I am completely and totally irresistible. But if you can rein yourself in long enough to finish this training session, I know you'll thank me come battle time."

I pushed away with a groan. "Is your ego your biggest feature, Andersson?"

"Oh, not by a long shot." Axel winked as he retrieved his weapon. "But we're taking things slow, Shieldmaiden. I'm not ready to show you my—whoa!"

Axel brought his knees to his chest as I swung low to the ground. He landed stealthily on his toes while I shifted my weight and attacked from the right. Then the left. Then the front. I kept moving, adjusting my angles until I'd driven him back to the wall. But he dropped onto the mat just as I lunged forward to pin his arms. Axel rolled swiftly to my right, leaping to his feet and pushing *me* into the wall from behind.

Dang it.

"Never repeat a pattern," he admonished. He ripped my stick from my hands and pinned my arms to the wall with his forearm. "You're better than that."

I really was. "Let's go again."

"It's cute that you think you can beat me," Axel taunted.

I narrowed my eyes as I flipped around to face him. "Just watch."

"Oh." He released my arms with a rakish grin. "I will."

For the next hour, we sparred with all the vigor of

19

two warriors who knew full well that they were up against a magic-wielding enemy. The next time we had a chance to capture our perp, we *had* to bring him in.

Our world literally depended on it.

CHAPTER 3

THE NEXT AFTERNOON, JANNA, Brigga, and
I hunkered down in a corner of the Kappa Mu
house library. We'd fallen behind on our mandatory
study hours, and we didn't want to give the sorority's
ethics chair/resident mean girl another reason to
torture us. Lexi had most definitely had it in for us
since our first day here. And while part of her ire may
have come from her disappointment that Axel just
wasn't that into her, it was equally possible she was just
really, really mean.

Some apples were simply rotten.

The "library" was actually a room in the down-
stairs portion of the Kappa Mu castle. There weren't
any books here—it was strictly a bring-your-own-
study-materials kind of place. Three long tables
stretched across its length, and two big windows
framed the outward-facing wall. They provided an
excellent view of the Alpha fraternity's backyard,

where what looked to be a glorious pool party was currently in full swing. Shirtless guys drank from red cups, occasionally abandoning their beverages to execute sloppy front flips into the water. They were surrounded by a bevy of girls wearing tiny triangles of material that barely covered their ample chests. Water-wear was definitely different in twenty-first century Los Angeles.

I was *so* never swimming here.

"Earth to Ingrid. You in there?" Brigga waved a delicate hand in front of my eyes.

"Huh? Sorry. I was just . . . uh . . ."

"Axel's not out there, if that's who you're looking for." A corner of Janna's lips shifted up. "I asked him and Raynor to do some recon on the geological museum—locate the loading dock, assess the layout to determine the likely location of Máni's orb, identify potential travel routes from the previous exhibit site."

"I wasn't looking for Axel." My words came out too quickly.

Janna shook her head. "Mmm-hmm."

"I wasn't! I was just . . . never mind." I picked up my pencil and tapped it to the parchment in my notebook. "Astronomy homework. That's where my focus is. On this group project—a four-page essay on the possible recurrence of an astrological alignment that hasn't been seen in centuries."

"A definite recurrence," Brigga corrected. "And one that more than likely accounts for the reason our dark mage showed up here and now—one thousand years in our future, and five thousand miles from his last known location."

"Read us what we have so far." Janna leaned back in her chair.

I framed my notebook with my forearms and read aloud. "During the Viking era, eight planets appeared in the same region of the sky. By all outward appearances, these planets were in alignment—an astronomical anomaly we now know to be impossible on account of the varied tilts of orbits and orientations. As the study of astronomy was less precise at that time, mankind believed this anomaly to be a magical channel from the heavens—a conduit by which energy could be funneled into objects and beings. Although such claims are scientifically unfounded, they have nonetheless resurfaced as the recurrence of the present-day alignment draws near. Next month, all eight planets will again appear to line up. And while it is unlikely that this phenomenon will lead to the lifting of the veil between the human and spirit worlds, the end of the world, or the creation of a super-weapon, as many now claim, the fact remains that such an event has been met with tremendous interest within the scientific and popular communities."

I turned the page.

"It sounds good so far," Janna praised.

"I'll give it another edit before we turn it in." Brigga frowned. "Keep reading."

"Okay." I looked back down. "New age healers are eager to see whether this year's alignment creates a cluster of super-crystals, similar to those allegedly formed during the previous occurrence. Folklore tells us that during the initial alignment, a group of minerals were struck by an energetic charge. These hyper-charged stones were imbued with traces of power that gave them the ability not only to heal, but to perform highly improbable tasks—what today would be called magic. While the existence of these 'magic rocks' has never been confirmed, they are none-theless the subject of great geological and astronomical curiosity."

"How many pages is that?" Brigga asked.

"Just two." I sighed. "We could go deeper into orbital paths or planetary tilts. Though Professor Stinoa's really into the cultural stuff, so maybe we should stick with the crystal angle instead."

"We could tie in what we read about the war between the mages," Janna offered. "I know it wasn't covered in class, but I bet she'd give us good marks if we were able to include cross-cultural references. Do we still have that library book on the mage war?"

"I think Raynor returned all the books last week. But I took notes. Hold on . . ." Brigga flipped through her parchment. "Ah, there it is. The war between the mages occurred during an astronomical anomaly—check—that created a surge of power—double check. The light mages wanted to harness the energy to protect the Earth, while the dark ones wanted to use it to open portals to dark realms. When the energy surged, it struck a massive crystal, imbuing it with mystical powers. The entire group promptly cast spells, destroying each other in their attempt to gain control of the crystal. One of the survivors shattered the crystal into a dozen pieces and scattered them across the land. He retreated into obscurity and was never heard from again."

I tapped my pencil to the desktop. "If that's true, it not only makes for a fascinating addendum to this paper, but it would explain our dark ma—"

"Hi, girls."

My spine stiffened as Kenzi walked through the doorway. *How much did she hear?*

"*Hei*, Kenzi." Janna smiled easily. "Are you here to log study hours, too?"

"I met my weekly quota yesterday." Kenzi pulled out a chair and joined us at our table. My nose twitched at the smell of whatever green liquid wafted from her travel cup. "I was just on my way out to pick up some sunscreen for tomorrow's beach exchange, and I wanted to see if you guys needed anything."

"That's really nice. Thanks, Kenzi. I think we're—"

"Well, well, well. If it isn't our resident defectors." The nasally voice of the girl I'd come to loathe pulled my eyes from Kenzi's questionable choice of tea. Lexi stood in the doorframe wearing her typical uniform—a short skirt and cropped shirt. Behind Lexi, her second-in-command smirked in a nearly identical outfit.

"Hello, Lexi. Becky." Janna's voice carried its typical calm. "I'm afraid we have no idea what you're talking about."

"Defectors?" Becky chimed in. "As in, you failed to attend last night's mandatory paintball exchange."

What the Helheim is a paintball?

"We had a folklore quiz today," Janna said easily. "We stayed home to prepare."

"So you find yourselves unable to keep on top of your studies. Is that what I'm hearing?" Lexi shook her head. "No wonder you're the only people in the library on a Friday afternoon. It must be *so hard* being exchange students. I mean, the classes here must be *so much tougher* than what you're used to in that little country of yours."

Did Lexi have something against Norway?

"I'm here too," Kenzi pointed out. "So it's not just them in the library."

"I'm afraid I have to write you up for your infraction." Lexi twirled one glossy curl around her pink-tipped finger. "The demerits alone will dock your curfew an hour—possibly two. So any dates you have this weekend will have to be—"

"Why are you writing them up?" Kenzi narrowed her eyes. "Exchanges have never been mandatory."

"They are when the entire social schedule was set around the arrival of three Norwegian exchange students." Lexi crossed her arms. "They're the reason the Lambdas put us on their calendar. You know we haven't had an exchange with them in two years. Our currency spiked when they found out we'd have actual Vikings living with us."

She had no idea. "Uh, thank you?"

"Still." Kenzi shook her head. "Exchanges aren't mandatory. Plenty of girls didn't show last night. Are you going to write them up, too?"

"Sure," Becky snarked.

"Really?" Kenzi pressed.

Lexi didn't blink.

"I'll check with my sister," Kenzi said. "If Kayla says *all* the girls who failed to attend are issued demerits, then I'll know you don't have it in for my friends. Because I'll be honest—I've seen you target these three from the minute they got here. And I know the ethics chair swore an oath of impartiality. So, if it turns out that you're showing favoritism . . . or un-favoritism, as it seems to be . . ."

Lexi shot eyeball daggers at our yoga instructor.

"Fine," she snapped. "I'll let you off with a warning. But next time, you'd *better* be there."

"Duly noted," Janna said calmly. "Though as Kenzi said, social events aren't exactly mandatory in the same way library and philanthropy hours are."

"Some are," Becky countered. "If you're not at the Winter Formal, you'll never get enough points to hold on to your triple room. Loads of girls want that one."

If we were still at Kappa Mu by the time of the Winter Formal, we'd be so far behind on our mission . . . I didn't even want to think about it.

My eyes met Lexi's, and she fired a fresh stream of hate-daggers my way. "Just make sure you're not embarrassing our house. We're one of the most sought-

27

after sororities on The Row. I'd hate for *someone* to jeopardize that."

"Don't you have a date to get ready for?" I leaned back in my chair. "Oh, right. If you're following up on ethics infractions, you *really* must not have anything better to do on a Friday night."

Lexi's eyes narrowed into thin slits. "Watch yourself, Inga. Challenging a superior officer is grounds for—"

"It's Ingrid," I said smoothly. "And if you'll excuse me, we need to finish our essay. Or are you infringing on the allocated study hours of a sister, in direct violation of Kappa Mu ordinance 7.1a?"

"You memorized the handbook?" Kenzi grinned.

"Of course I did." I was on a mission, after all.

"Come on, Becky." Lexi turned on one heel and stormed down the hall. Her minion shot us a haughty look before flouncing after her.

"Ugh." I rolled my eyes. "She is the *worst.*"

"Agreed." Janna sighed. "Is she like that to everyone?"

"Yes. No. Both." Kenzi laughed. "Lexi's always been a pain, but she seems to really have it in for you guys. What did you do to set her off?"

"I think Ingrid took her favorite toy away from her." Brigga giggled. "A tall, muscular, man-bun wearing toy named Axel Andersson."

"I didn't take anything." I picked up my pencil. "Axel was never hers to begin with—and if he'd been into . . . *that.*" I shuddered. "Well, just ick."

"Agreed." Kenzi toyed with the beaded bracelets on her wrist. "But you should probably do something to cleanse your auras. Lexi just flung some seriously bad juju your way."

"I'm sure we're fine." No way did I want to go through *another* one of Kenzi's yoga workouts. My abs were still screaming from this morning's ninety-minute core session. Who knew "stretching" was so hard?

"You're not fine." Kenzi raised her hands so they framed my abdomen. "Ingrid, Lexi's set something directly inside of your second chakra. Makes sense if she's into your boyfriend, since that region's connected to your . . . intimacy."

What?

"Janna, you've got what looks like cobwebs in your third—from what I can tell, Lexi's messing with your personal power." Kenzi shifted her attention to Brigga. "And you have . . . huh. You're pretty clear."

"Lexi doesn't see Brigga as a threat?" I chuckled.

Brigga's lips turned downward. "Ingrid!"

"It's probably because she knows you're into Raynor, so you're not potential Axel competition," I offered. "Wait, you and Raynor *are* together, right?"

"Raynor and I are . . ." Brigga bit on her bottom lip. "We're exploring something new. Slowly."

"Ah." Kenzi nodded. "Well, either way, you're all welcome to join me at the Spiritual Center for Meditation on Sunday. I'm doing a day-long retreat to purify my chakras."

Uh . . .

"Is Kayla going with you?" Janna asked.

"My sister's taking a hike with Mike." Kenzi leaned in and lowered her voice. "Just between us, I think he's going to pin her."

"Pin her?" Was Kayla's boyfriend her sparring partner, too?

"Do they not do that in Oslo?" Kenzi glanced over her shoulder. "Pinning is like a pre-engagement ceremony. The guy asks the girl to wear his fraternity pin, and if she accepts, we do a whole candlelight thing with both houses present. It's a pretty big deal."

"Wow." Brigga's eyes lit up. "That sounds so romantic!"

"It's nice," Kenzi agreed. "A little extreme for my tastes, though. How can you know who you want to spend your life with when you've barely even begun to discover who you are? I realize people marry young in some parts of the world, but in California we don't really do that until we're thirty. For the guys, older."

"You don't choose a partner until you're *thirty?*" Brigga squeaked. "That's ancient!"

"Not here it's not." Kenzi laughed. "So, I guess you guys do it earlier in Norway?"

"It varies," I said carefully. I had no idea what people did *now*, but marriages in Valkyris happened a few years after you graduated from the academy. Twenty seemed to be the norm there. *Or then.*

"I guess every situation is different." Kenzi pushed her chair back. "Anyway, think about my offer—the guru himself will be leading Sunday's retreat. He's been gone for a while, so we're really excited to have him back. His energy is just so . . . pure." Kenzi sighed dreamily.

"The guru's good-looking, isn't he?" Janna deduced.

"Extremely," Kenzi confirmed. "Just think about it."

"We will. Thanks, Kenzi."

"No worries." With a wave, Kenzi pushed in her chair and glided from the room.

"So?" I grinned at Janna. "Want to meditate *all day long*?"

"Uh . . . not particularly." She glanced at her parchment. "We'd better finish up this paper. If we're late for dinner, gods only know what Lexi will do to us."

"Maybe we really should cleanse our . . . what did she call it?" Brigga pursed her lips. "Our goo-goo?"

"Juju," I corrected. "And no thanks. If Kenzi's meditation center is anything like her yoga workouts, I'd need a week to recover. Axel's already kicking my butt in our training sessions. I don't need to give him any advantages."

Janna frowned. "He's *not* a better trainer than I am."

"Definitely not," I agreed. "Even if he thinks he is. But he's ridiculously good at anticipating our patterns. If I run a routine on him *one time*, he locks it into his memory."

"That's an impressive defense." Admiration colored Janna's tone. "And it's rare, but it does happen in the field. All the more reason for us to draw up new offensive routines."

"Maybe," I agreed. "But first, this paper. Brigga, what's the best way to work in the folklore angle?"

"Let me see that." Brigga pulled my notebook across the table and studied the pages. "Got it. We can include a secondary cultural section below the main text and finish with the planetary orbit pattern. Or vice versa. Hmm. Maybe if . . ."

As our disseminator worked out the best way to impress Professor Stinoa, I let my gaze drift back to the window. The Alphas and their guests were having the time of their lives jumping into the pool, drinking, and laughing as if a dark mage wasn't about to destroy their world. *And obliterate mine.*

Gods willing, we could stop our target's plan . . . before he managed to set it in motion.

CHAPTER 4

"OKAY, LISTEN UP! I'M only going to say this once, so shut up already!"

Lexi stood at the front of the bus, her hands cupped around her mouth. Her cheeks pinked as the Alphas let out a series of whistles and claps.

"You tell 'em, Lexi!"

"Ooh, teacher's getting mad!"

"Uh-oh! Don't wanna set her off!"

"Shut up!" Lexi yelled again.

The bevy of boys laughed before resuming their animated conversations. My gaze darted between the crowded beach parking lot and the angry ethics chairwoman. Lexi had been on my case all morning, criticizing my hair, my outfit, and the cleanliness of my room. She was determined to give me a demerit for whatever imagined infraction she could conjure, and as fun as it was to see my nemesis lose her cool, if these guys set her off, she'd only take it out on me.

I turned to my seatmate with a reluctant sigh. "Axel? A little help?"

"I thought you hated her." Axel jutted his chin toward the front of the bus.

"Valkyrians hate no one," I said serenely. "Our love extends to all."

"Ingrid. Please." Axel smoothed the front of his wildly patterned shirt. *Hawaiian*, one of the guys had called it. To me, it was just *so very bright*. "I know you better than that."

"Okay, fine. She's awful. But she'll get worse if they make her mad. You never poke a bear."

"Gods, no," Axel agreed. He raised his voice. "Come on, guys. Ease up. Let the lady talk so we can all go to the beach already."

"Thank you, Axel." Lexi batted her eyelashes as the noise dropped a decibel. *Mother Frigga.* "As I was saying, we're all here to have fun. But fun comes with rules, so let's go over ours."

"Crack that whip," the guy in front of us hollered.

"Leave Lex alone," a curly haired Alpha yelled.

The first guy ignored him. "Hey, Lexi, you wanna go out sometime? You know I'm into girls who—"

Axel reached forward and smacked the idiot on the head.

"Why'd you do that, man?" The guy turned around with a frown. Like Axel, he wore a bright floral shirt.

"Show the lady some respect," Axel admonished.

"Easy for you to say." The guy shifted his gaze to me. His eyes ran slowly down my body before settling

34

on the *V*-shaped neck of my sundress. "You've already got yourself a hot piece of—"

His words were stopped by a swift fist to his face. *Mine.*

"Ow!" He rubbed his nose. "Axel, get your girlfriend in check."

"I don't control her," Axel chuckled. "And I'd say she's got things well in check herself."

"She hit me!"

"You deserved it," Axel said honestly.

The guy pulled his hand from his face, checking for blood. "That was hard!"

"I should hope so," Axel said. "Her trainer is a stickler for technique. Pretty impressive teacher, that one."

"Please," I scoffed. "I knew that move *way* before I ever met you."

"Well," he hedged. "Maybe. But the combination of everything *else* I taught you no doubt contributed to your—"

"If you all don't shut up right now, we are never getting off this bus!" Lexi's cheeks had turned a deep shade of red.

Oops.

"Thank you," she muttered as the chatter died down. "Now, here's the deal. We've reserved a spot to the right of the pier. It's behind the lifeguard stations in a section roped off with red and gold tape. Help yourselves to anything in the coolers and catering trays— we went with Mexican food, and gluten-free and vegan options are available so be sure to ask the servers if you have any dietary restrictions. Alcohol will be in the blue cooler, and I'm legally obligated to say it's only for those over twenty-one—"

"Boo!" the chorus erupted.

"I said it was a legal obligation, okay?" Lexi snapped. "Red coolers have non-alcoholic options. I'll be handing out ride wristbands and game tokens as you leave the bus—pier management is testing a new system with the vendors this weekend, and you can use the tokens instead of cash to play the carnival games. Be back here no later than nine—we're leaving for campus then, and anyone who's not on the bus *will* be left behind. Any questions? *Eek!*"

Lexi jumped backward as the Alphas and Kappas moved as one—a sea of bodies surging for the door.

"I guess it's time." Axel stood, and offered me his hand. I laced my fingers through his, heat slowly moving up my arm and into my belly as he winked. Behind me, Brigga and Raynor waited patiently for the mob to pass.

"Ready for the beach?" Janna asked from across the aisle.

"I guess." I glanced out the window, toward the edge of the parking lot. "This looks nothing like the ones back home. Where are all the rocks?"

"We have sand beaches in Norway," Brigga pointed out.

"None that I've ever seen," I countered.

"They're there," Raynor confirmed. He stepped into

the aisle as it cleared. "More in the southern regions though. It's rougher on the island."

"That makes sense." I let Axel lead me to the front of the bus. "I've never been south of Valkyris."

"It's nice." Janna fell into step behind me. "I'll bring you on the next squad mission that takes us that way."

"Sounds good." I followed Axel, Raynor, and Brigga down the steps and into the sunshine.

Lexi stood in the parking lot, distributing tokens. "Here you go, Raynor. Brigga. Axel." It was impossible not to notice the way Lexi pushed out her chest as she passed Axel his wristband. "Here, take some extra tokens. That's for *trying* to stand up for me back there."

"Anytime." Axel winked. "You might want to thank Jack, too. He looked ready to rip into Trevor."

"Is that so?" Lexi glanced over her shoulder. The curly-haired Alpha from the bus shot her an easy grin. "Hmm. I'll have to look into that."

"Hey," I objected as she walked away. "What about my tokens?"

"And mine?" Janna chimed in.

"Here." Lexi tossed a small bag, and I snatched it from the air. She was halfway across the parking lot by the time I extracted two wristbands and passed one to Janna.

"Guess she's off duty," I said.

"Guess so." Axel snaked his arm around my shoulders. "What do you say? Should we hit the beach or the pier or—"

"I want to see *that*." Janna pointed to the huge, illuminated wheel that sat atop the walkway. It spun slowly, stopping at regular intervals for gods only knew what reason.

"I think that's their *Ferris wheel*," Raynor offered.

"Their what?" Axel fastened the plastic strip around his wrist. I did the same.

"It's a ride," Brigga said. "They sit in those little compartments and go in a big circle. It's the world's only solar-powered Ferris wheel, and since they harness the power from the sun, it's an energy-efficient solution they're hoping will catch on in other recreational facilities."

"How do you know all of this?" I handed Janna a fistful of tokens.

"I'm our disseminator, Ingrid," Brigga reminded me. "It's my *job* to know all of this."

"Right." I tucked the remainder of the tokens into the small pack I wore on my back. "Well, I guess we're going to the Ferris wheel. Looks like the pier entrance is up there."

"Lead the way." Axel gestured with one arm, and I marched us across the parking lot. When my short dress fluttered in the light breeze, I awkwardly tugged it down.

Stupid dress.

"You okay?" Axel asked.

"*Ja.*" I sighed. "Just not loving what passes for beach attire in this era."

"I happen to like your beach attire very much." Axel's eyes slid to my vast expanse of exposed leg.

"Watch it," I warned.

"What? I'm not allowed to appreciate the traditional folk costumes of contemporary Los Angelenians?"

"Los Angelinos," Brigga corrected from behind.

"Whatever." Axel's eyes hadn't left my legs.

"Don't make me punch you, too," I warned.

"Fine." Axel grinned. "Save your right hook for the training room. Or maybe the games—look at that."

I followed his point to the end of the pier. The first booth housed the figure of a bear with a sign that read, "Test Your Strength!"

"Beat the beast and win a prize," Janna read. "Hmm. That could be interesting."

"There's something wrong with that bear," Raynor whispered.

"It's inflatable," Brigga offered. "They blow things up with a special kind of air, and they float. Or not— some things they blow up to bounce on. Like that."

We all looked in the direction she gestured. An enormous castle stood near the water where a group of children jumped happily across its surface.

"Holy Mother Frigga," Janna murmured. "That's made of air?"

"The inside is," Brigga confirmed. "They call them *bounce houses.*"

Axel's face lit up. "Los Angeles is fun."

"When it's not under siege by a dark mage," I muttered.

"Aw, come on, Ingrid." Axel nudged me with his shoulder. "You're off duty tonight."

"Technically speaking, shieldmaidens are *never* off duty," I corrected.

"She's not wrong," Janna agreed. "And as head of the Airborne Assassins, I'd think you'd—"

"Okay! I get it. We're all on the clock, at all times. Which is why we're all carrying weapons, *ja?*" Axel patted the waistband of his swimsuit, which I knew concealed his travel dagger.

"Of course." My own dagger was strapped to my thigh. It had taken me a hot minute to find a dress long enough to at least hide the blade. *Stupid contemporary folk costumes . . .*

"But we already know our target's sitting tight until a week from Wednesday. That's the day the exhibit's being delivered to the museum, which will *also* be the day that Máni's moonstone will be the most vulnerable to theft." Axel's fingers wove through mine. "So can we *please* go challenge that weird-looking bear? I want to see it take Raynor down."

"Hey," Raynor objected.

"We all know you're not the strongest fighter here." Axel smirked. "That honor goes to me."

"Uh, excuse me," I said. "I do believe *I* kicked *your* butt in training yesterday."

"I remember no such thing."

My eyes narrowed. "Oh, it's on, Andersson. I'm going to destroy you at the bear challenge."

"Not if I destroy you first."

"Do you two have to compete over *everything?*" Brigga groaned.

"Yes." Axel and I spoke in unison.

"Ugh. Fine." Brigga stomped toward the pier. "But afterwards, we *are* going on that Ferris wheel."

"Race you to the bear booth," I challenged. I dropped Axel's hand and took off at a sprint.

"Cheater!" he shouted from behind.

With a laugh, I charged toward the pier. Axel was right—we could take *one* afternoon off. We had a plan, a likely procurement date for our target, and a week and a half before the real work began. We deserved a little fun.

Gods knew we needed it.

CHAPTER 5

AXEL EMERGED VICTORIOUS IN our bear battle. But I trounced him in the archery game. And Janna beat us all in the arm-wrestling competition.

"How did you get so good at this?" I panted as the mechanical arm pinned my fist to the table for a third time.

"How do you think Ethel and I entertain ourselves?" Janna arched one brow.

"You guys arm wrestle? That's your idea of fun?" I massaged my aching hand.

"You're one to talk." Janna waved her hand. "You and Axel try to kill each other daily."

"That's *work*," I countered.

"It's fun, too." Axel wiped the sweat from my brow. "Especially when I pin your arms to the mat and you—"

"Hey, girls! Fancy meeting you here." Kenzi's lyrical voice halted Axel's over-share. I shot her a grateful grin as she glided across the boardwalk, her gauzy dress fluttering against her thighs.

"*Hei*, Kenzi." Brigga waved. "Have you tried this one yet? Ingrid's awful at it."

"It's hard," I objected.

"I'm actually pretty good at arm wrestling," Kenzi said confidently. "Yoga is excellent at improving wrist strength."

"Apparently sword fighting isn't," Axel muttered.

"What's that?" Kenzi asked.

"Axel was just saying he's bad at this one too," I said.

"That is not what I—"

"Axel should come to my morning workout." Kenzi grinned. "We could take it outside if you want to join us. Maybe do a little core work."

"What's wrong with my core?" Axel looked down at his stomach. Which, I knew from the other day's shirtless run, needed absolutely *zero work*.

Mmm, Axel's abs . . .

Focus, Ingrid.

"Since you're all here, I wanted to introduce you to my guru, Torstein. I had no idea he'd be at the pier today, but we bumped into each other at the frozen-yogurt stand and, well, here he is."

I tore my eyes away from Axel's torso, and focused on the man standing next to Kenzi. He was tall—easily six-and-a-half feet. Long, blond hair hung loose around thick biceps that strained against the short sleeves of his white, linen shirt. His lightly tanned skin glowed with health, and he stared back at me with eyes that matched the pale-blue sky.

This was Kenzi's meditation teacher?

"Torstein, these are my sorority sisters—the ones from Norway that I told you about. Ingrid, Janna, and Brigga." Kenzi pointed to each of us in turn. "And these are their friends, Axel and Raynor. They're all here on an exchange program."

"Ah. Ingrid, is it?" Torstein reached out to clasp my hands between his. A jolt shot up my arm as he pressed his palms to my skin, closed his eyes, and bowed. "Namaste."

What the Helheim was that?

"Namaste," I repeated.

Axel shifted beside me.

"*Hei*. I'm Axel." My boyfriend's voice was slightly louder than normal. "It's good to meet you, man."

"Axel." Torstein shifted his attention. "The divine in me greets the divine in you. Hmm. That's curious."

"What is?" Axel asked.

"You seem familiar. Have we met?"

"Pretty sure I'd remember that." Axel slipped his arm around my shoulders. He didn't take his eyes off Torstein's hands. They hadn't released mine. And the pulse shooting up my arm hadn't decreased *at all*.

This is beyond awkward.

"I'm Janna." My captain saved me by sticking out her arm. I exhaled as Torstein opened his palms and the tingling stopped. *Thank gods.*

"It's lovely to meet you, Janna." Torstein shook her hand. "It's lovely to meet *all* of you."

"Did Kenzi say you're a *goo-roo*?" Raynor frowned. "What is that, exactly?"

"I loathe the phrase myself." Torstein raked his fingers through his glossy, golden strands. "It calls to the ego, which is destined to be shed—released to fertilize the earth like the absolute waste that it is."

"Nonetheless, you *are* our guru." Kenzi turned to Raynor. "Torstein is the head of the Spiritual Center for Meditation. We have three campuses now—he just opened one in San Diego, though most of our members prefer the Malibu location."

"The chi is strongest there." Torstein's tone had a musical lilt—the slight accent of the Nordic countries evident in his voice. "The tidal alignments are particularly intense at full moon, and crystal therapies have been especially effective."

Axel's eyes narrowed. "Where exactly are you from?"

"Torstein grew up in Norway, too," Kenzi offered. "He came to America to share the spiritual practices he developed after spending ten years in solitude in a forest."

"Really?" Axel sounded doubtful.

I didn't exactly blame him. Torstein didn't look a day over twenty-five. Which would mean he'd been on his own since, well, before he was of legal age . . . in this era, at least.

"Silence and solitude unlock our truths," Torstein

said serenely. "Though, of course, I am pleased to once again be among my fellow cosmic travelers."

O-kay . . .

"These are the girls I practice yoga with every morning." Kenzi gestured to Janna, Brigga, and I. "I invited them to the meditation retreat on Sunday, but I think they've already got plans, so—"

"We'll be there," Brigga blurted.

I glanced over to find her staring adoringly at Torstein. She'd pulled her shoulders back and now angled her chest toward the guru while she furiously batted her eyelashes. Beside her, Raynor folded his arms across his chest.

"We will?" I glanced at Janna.

My captain just shrugged.

"Yes." Brigga beamed. "I meant to tell you, Kenzi, we checked our schedules and we don't have plans after all. So we will *definitely* join you."

"Wonderful." Torstein folded his hands together in prayer. "I look forward to the convening of our spirits."

"You're going to love the center," Kenzi said. "It's up on the bluffs, and every room has at least one full glass wall that faces the ocean, so the views are pristine. It's just sea air, and open space, and nature, and peace. It's perfection."

"I'll bet," Raynor said drily.

Torstein slid his calm gaze across our group. He zeroed in on me as he said, "It will be my pleasure to enter the serene state of oneness with you."

A bizarre tingling broke out along my spine. *What the Helheim?*

"Thank you." Janna stepped forward. "Well, we'd better get going. We promised Brigga a trip on the Ferris wheel, and she gets cranky if we don't follow the agenda."

"No, I don't!" Brigga objected.

"We'll see you tomorrow, Torstein." Janna nodded. "Kenzi."

"Have fun." Kenzi waved. "Focus on the horizon if you get dizzy up there."

"Will do." Axel didn't take his eyes off of Torstein as the guru led Kenzi along the pier. When their figures had blended into the crowd, he turned to me with a frown. "I don't trust that guy."

"Kenzi's meditation teacher? Why not?"

"There's just something . . . off about him."

"He lived in a forest for ten years, Axel." Brigga shook her head. "The poor thing is probably just reacclimating to human contact."

"Exactly. Why would he come to one of the most populated cities in the modern world if he'd only ever had bears to keep him company?"

"Axel's right," Raynor said. "Torstein's weird."

"Don't worry, boys," Janna said. "I'll keep an eye on these two—make sure they don't run off with the gorgeous guru."

"Janna!" Brigga blushed.

"Anyone can see that he's attractive," Janna said drily. "But I'm with Axel and Raynor on this one.

47

There's something not right there. What do you think, Ingrid?"

I didn't want to admit to what I'd felt—the electric shock the guru's touch had sent up my arm, or the weird tingles his too-intense gaze had sparked along my back. So, I just shrugged and said, "He's definitely out there. I didn't get a bad feeling from him, though."

Just a slightly overheated one.

"Well, I don't trust him," Axel reiterated. "But I do trust you and Janna to take care of yourselves . . . and Brigga."

"Hey," Brigga objected. "I can hold my own."

"Axel." I shook my head. "It's not like the yoga guy is going to attack anyone. Worst he could do is Namaste us to sleep. I always pass out during Kenzi's end-of-class meditations."

"You and me both," Janna agreed.

As we headed toward the Ferris wheel, I glanced at Axel. His brows were knitted together, and tension radiated from the arm he'd draped around my shoulders. "You all right, Andersson?"

"I'm fine." He wiped the scowl from his face and brushed his lips against my forehead. "Just be careful tomorrow, okay?"

"I always am," I reminded him. "Now, come on. Maybe I'll win you one of those stuffed dragons after we ride the Ferris wheel. Odin only knows how much you miss yours."

Axel shook his head. "Everything's easier when you have a dragon."

"Agree to disagree." I shuddered at the memory of the massive, fire-breathing beasts that Axel wrangled back home. "Those creatures are absolutely terrifying."

"So were you when I met you." Axel brushed an errant curl behind my ear.

"I still am." I leveled him with a stare.

"Of course." He nodded seriously. "Especially when you're getting your butt handed to you by a mechanical, wrestling arm."

"I could have beat it if I wanted to," I muttered.

"Of course you could have," Axel said. "I'd never bet against you."

"Good."

"Except in arm wrestling."

My fist connected with his shoulder. He laughed as he wrapped his hand around mine and pulled me toward the Ferris wheel. While we waited in line, I rested my head against his shoulder and sighed happily. So much of our life was chaotic, it was nice to have a day to just relax.

Even if we knew it couldn't last.

CHAPTER 6

"OH. MY. GODS. AXEL, look. That man has a small dragon."

A little piece of Valkyris was just sitting on the Santa Monica Pier in all its green and spiky and, Odin willing, *not* fire-breathing glory. How was this even possible?

"What? Where?" Axel dug his heels into the boardwalk and whipped his head from side to side. The rest of our group had gone down to the beach to grab some food while I thoroughly defeated Axel at the beanbag toss. Following his humiliation, he'd announced that he refused to be sport-shamed by his girlfriend and set out to win me the biggest prize on the pier—a three-foot tall stuffed polar bear with glittery eyes and "I Heart L.A." stamped across its back. It had taken him thirty minutes of throwing balls into jugs, not to mention countless muttered curse words—both in this language *and* our own—but he'd sworn it had been worth it to, and I quote, "Wipe that ridiculous smirk off your face, Shieldmaiden."

It was cute. In an egotistical warrior kind of way. *Snort.*

"Where is the small dragon?" Axel repeated.

"Over there." I pointed to my right.

A bald, tattooed man sat with his back to the railing. Across his shoulders stretched a tiny dragon. Its body was easily two-feet in length, with an equally long tail, and spikes that ran the full length of its back. It was perfectly still except for the slight flicker of its neck with each breath. I'd never seen anything like it.

Not on this scale at least.

Axel's breath hitched as he zeroed in on the reptile. "Mother Frigga. What is it?"

"Maybe they miniaturize their dragons in the next —er, *last* thousand years. That would explain why Freia didn't want us to bring one with us. It would have stood out among its . . . considerably smaller descendants."

"Do you think he'll let me pet it?"

I transferred my enormous, stuffed bear to the crook of one arm. "Do you let people touch *your* dragons?"

"The other handlers that work with them, sure. It takes a village to raise a dragon."

"But do you let total strangers interact with them?" I asked.

"Well. No." Axel lifted one shoulder. "But it's worth a shot."

Here we go.

"*Hei*, man." Axel approached the reptile handler. "If you don't mind my asking—what kind of dragon is that?"

"Dragon? I like that." The man nodded to himself. "This dragon's an iguana. His name's Rufus."

"Would you mind if I . . ." Axel reached one hand toward the animal.

"Not at all. You can hold him if you want to."

"Really?" Axel's face lit up like a kid at Winter Solstice. His hands trembled slightly as the man removed the reptile from his shoulders and raised it over Axel's open arms.

"You ever held a lizard before?" the man questioned.

Double snort.

Axel Andersson was the commander of a legion of warriors whose primary mode of transportation were this creature's winged, fire-breathing, oversized reptilian cousins. Axel had done things on lizards this man couldn't have imagined, from waging wars on militant tribes to battling the reanimated armies of the not-quite-dead. But for once, he kept his ego in check and simply said, "*Ja.*"

"You just seem nervous." The man arched one bushy brow.

"It's been a while, is all." Axel's voice wavered. "I used to have, uh, a few of these guys."

"You asked me what Rufus was." The handler's eyes narrowed.

"Axel owned a different species," I jumped in. "His were slightly larger."

"You owned Komodo dragons?" The man looked impressed.

Sure, we'd go with that.

"Keep him steady," he warned. "His back end can be squirrelly, so watch out for the—"

Axel chuckled as Rufus whipped his tail onto Axel's forearm.

"The tail," the handler finished. "Sorry about that. You okay?"

"I've had worse," Axel said. "So you're one of those, eh, Rufus?"

"He'll make you work for it." The man settled the lizard in Axel's arms. "But he's a big softie under his thick, stubborn skin."

"I can see that." Axel's lips rose at the corners. He lifted the iguana to look it in the eye. "*Hei*, Rufus. I'm Axel. Look at those talons. You're tough, aren't you?"

The Airborne Assassin was talking to a lizard. We'd officially hit *that* level of crazy.

"You really like him, eh?" The man rubbed lightly at his neck.

"I've raised reptiles for years. Trained them into highly skilled . . . uh, pets. A handful have even imprinted on me." Axel scratched Rufus' chin. The lizard's eyes rolled closed. "But I don't have any at the moment. Sure do miss them, though. They're great animals—inherently intelligent. Loyal. Forces of nature when they—"

"Ahem." I cleared my throat. I wasn't sure where Axel was going with this.

"Right." Axel stroked the spikes along Rufus' spine. "Like I said, I'm a big fan."

"Do you want one?" the man asked.

"I wish," Axel said.

"I mean it. My landlord won't let me keep Rufus. I brought him to the pier hoping I'd find a new owner. Have his terrarium with me and everything."

"His what?" I followed the man's gaze to the massive glass cage at his side. "Oh. His house?"

"What else?" The man didn't take his eyes off Axel. "So, you want him?"

Axel's eyes slid toward me. "What do you think?"

"Is that his . . . uh, his full size?" I asked.

"He may grow a few more inches, but I think he's pretty much done," the man said. "Come on. He likes you."

I studied Rufus. Sure enough, with Axel now rubbing his cheek, the lizard practically preened. His chin tilted up, and it looked as if he was *smiling*.

This day had turned real weird, real fast.

"You're sure it won't get you kicked out of the Alpha house?" I pressed.

"We can have animals there," Axel said. "One guy has a bird. And there are some fish."

"Well, then . . ."

"So, you'll keep him?" the man asked.

Axel grinned. "I'll take him off your hands. *Ja.*"

"Great." Rufus' handler pushed himself to his feet.

"He's still young, so feed him once a day. Leaves, fruits, vegetables—I'm sure you know the drill. Terrarium and heat lamp are there. He's not leash-trained or anything, so keep him inside—or watch him closely if you let him go out. Cool?"

Axel met the man's eyes. "I'll take good care of this animal. You have my word."

"Axel's great with reptiles," I offered.

And he was. With the larger, wing-bearing, flame-prone kinds.

But this stranger didn't need to know that.

"Well, goodbye then." The man scratched Rufus' back. "Take care, my friend." With a nod, he spun on his heel and disappeared into the crowd.

I turned to Axel. "Did you really just adopt a lizard?"

"Iguana, Ingrid." Axel shifted the animal to his shoulders. "Rufus is an iguana."

"Sure." Rufus draped himself contentedly across Axel's thick shoulders. When Axel bent carefully to lift the terrarium, I said, "Need a hand with that?"

"I've got it," he grunted. "It's not heavy, just awkward."

"You're walking around with a lizard on your neck."

"Yes. I am." Axel headed to the end of the boardwalk and turned for the sand.

I followed alongside him, checking every few seconds to make sure nothing fell out of the cage.

"Man, I missed these guys. They're such a huge part of my life. I know this mission won't take long in the big picture, but, well . . ."

"I get it. Being someone you're not is hard."

Axel looked over to me. "How are you handling everything?"

"I'll be better after we catch our target. I've never had to track someone who can just disappear into thin air." I sighed. "But we know what site he's hitting next. That's a plus. And I know you and Raynor set up a stakeout schedule, so at least we've got a plan."

"We do," Axel confirmed. "And it's a good one. The artifacts are currently in a museum about four hundred miles from here. They'll arrive via armored transport one week from Wednesday. We'll set up watch the night before, wait for our mage to show, and boom. We'll be on the next dagger-beam home, target in custody and life back to normal."

"And is Rufus coming along with us?"

Axel grinned at the now sleeping lizard. "I'm sure the dragons will adopt him—make him a junior member of the clan. They're inclusive like that."

"Mmm-hmm." My gaze wandered down the beach to the spot where a young family played in the sand. The woman rolled a ball toward a tiny boy, while the man picked up a girl with bright, crimson curls and spun her in a dizzying circle. She squealed with laughter before crying, "Again, Daddy! Again!"

"You all right?" Axel asked.

"Huh? Yeah. I just, uh . . ." My heart tugged as I clutched my stuffed prize to my chest. This family was so happy. So at ease. Just playing together, enjoying each other—appreciating this time for the gift they'd chosen to make it. It was simple, and pure, and everything I'd ever wanted. When in reality . . .

"Oh. *Oh.*" I caught Axel's movement in the corner of my eye. But I couldn't stop staring at the little girl. Her playful giggle. Her wild hand claps. Her unadulterated . . . *joy.*

She was exactly as she should be.

"Look at me, Shieldmaiden." Axel's hand on my arm broke my focus.

"Mmm?"

"Hey." Axel stepped over the now grounded terrarium. "I'm sorry you didn't get that."

"It's fine," I said automatically.

"No. It's not fine." Axel's hands framed my shoulders. "You should have had a family like that. You *deserved* a family like that."

"That's the thing about families, isn't it?" I locked in on Axel's emerald stare. "You can't control what you're born into."

"Maybe," Axel agreed. "But you *do* get to choose what happens once you're here. You got a bad deal, no way to spin it. But you took that deal and turned it into something amazing. You fight for Valkyris now. You live among people who dedicate their lives to ensuring that nobody grows up in a village like yours was. Who view our entire clan as one big family—a family they *choose* to be a part of every single day."

"I know," I whispered. "I'm so grateful I got to join Valkyris when I rescued you from Clan Bjorn."

"*I* rescued *you*," Axel corrected.

"Who rowed our boat all the way home?"

"Who broke you out of the slave hut?"

"Who got our escape-dragon killed?"

"Shh." Axel glanced at the lizard on his shoulder. "You'll scare Rufus."

"He's property of an assassin now. Maybe he should be a little scared."

"My point is"—Axel squeezed my shoulders —"there's the family you're born into. And there's the family you chose. You chose Valkyris. You chose your friends. You chose the Shieldmaiden Squadron. And because you must be slightly crazy, you chose me. And I swear to you, Ingrid, I will be for you what you never had but always deserved. I'll be your rock. Your safe harbor. Your stability. I will adore you with every bit of my being and tell you every single day how remarkable you truly are. I will back you in every conflict, champion every cause you believe in, and be by your side in every battle. I *will* protect you, Shieldmaiden. From every hurt in every era, in all the worlds."

My heart swelled with happiness. *Gods, this man . . .*

"I don't need protecting," I said softly.

"I know you don't." Axel spoke firmly. "It's one of the things I respect the most about you."

My pulse quickened as Axel leaned forward to touch his forehead to mine.

"I swear to Odin, Ingrid, I will be everything you need me to be. Today. Tomorrow. One thousand years from now—and one thousand years before now. I'll be right here, at your side, for as long as you'll have me."

"I know you will," I whispered. "That's one of the things I respect the most about *you.*"

"Good." Axel brushed his lips against mine, and I dropped my stuffed bear onto the sand. A low groan rumbled from Axel's chest as he slipped his hands around my waist. He pulled me so close, I could feel his heartbeat beneath the thin fabric of my sundress. I slid one hand beneath Axel's shirt. The corded muscles of his back were taut, and as I traced them with my fingertips, a slow heat built in my belly. I dug my sandals into the sand and stood on tiptoe, pressing myself against Axel so that nothing but a light layer of cotton separated us. He settled his palm at the base of my spine and flexed his hips into mine, sending a fresh wave of warmth coursing through me. My nails dug into his skin, my breath shuddering as Axel nipped lightly at my upper lip. He ran his tongue along the bite, pain replacing pleasure. I sighed contentedly as Axel deepened the kiss. As I slid my hand up his back, Axel dipped me lower in his arms. My head tilted, and he traced the line of my neck with soft kisses that grew in intensity as he made his way lower. By the time he reached my collarbone, a fierce shiver ripped through me. It was too much and not enough all at the same time. I withdrew my hand from Axel's shirt and brought it to his cheek, savoring the rough fibers of his beard between my fingertips as I guided his mouth to mine. He raked my bottom lip between his teeth, sending a fresh surge roaring due south.

Why the Helheim did I wait to so long to let myself fall for this man?

I could have stayed right there, kissing Axel on that beach forever.

"Ouch!" I winced as a thick tail slapped my bicep. I stared Axel's new pet down. "Rufus, no," I said firmly. "No tail flicking."

"Don't move." Axel lifted the lizard from his shoulders and set him inside the glass cage. He carefully placed the lid before sliding his arms around my waist and pulling my hips to his. "Now," he said as he pressed his lips lightly to mine, "where were we?"

"Get a room, Andersson!" A series of catcalls interrupted what was sure to be another unforgettable kiss.

"Shut up," Axel called back.

With a sigh, I tipped my head to the darkening sky. "We should probably go join them. The food will be gone if we wait any longer."

"Mmm." Axel's thumb ran slow circles against my spine. "You hungry?"

"A little," I admitted. "Plus, I don't like your housemates watching while we . . . well . . ."

"I get it." Axel's hand slipped around my side. He ran his fingers up my arm and cupped my face in his massive palm. "But the minute I get you alone, Shieldmaiden . . ."

I rose on my toes to whisper in his ear, "Promise?"

He groaned. "Gods, yes."

"Good." I pressed my lips to his jaw, shivering at the way his beard tickled my skin. "Now, we'd better go before Rufus breaks out of that cage. Something tells me he's going to be a handful."

"Sounds like someone I know." Axel drew me in for one more kiss.

"Watch it, Andersson." I pulled back with a laugh before picking up my stuffed bear and marching toward the party.

"Oh. I'm watching." Axel's eyes had shifted to my butt. Beside him, Rufus' tail slapped fiercely against the side of his cage.

"Your lizard is angry," I called out.

"Rufus. None of that." Axel glanced lovingly at the little green monster. I smiled as he lifted the carrier and lectured his pet about the importance of patience, respect, and mutual understanding. I'd never gotten his affinity for scaly, fork-tongued animals, but he looked so happy to be reunited with something familiar, albeit in a smaller, flame-free form.

Warmth filled my chest as my fierce assassin made silly faces at his new pet. I was falling for Axel just a little bit more with each passing day. And hearing him say he believed in me; that he wanted to be my champion without undermining my own strength . . .

It looked like we'd *both* gotten something we needed today.

CHAPTER 7

SIX A.M. CAME MUCH faster than I'd anticipated. My vision was still blurry as I dragged myself out of bed and settled into the back of Kenzi's car for our hour-long drive to Malibu. For once, the freeways were uncrowded. Apparently, the residents of Los Angeles didn't rise merrily at dawn on Sundays.

"Here we are. The Spiritual Center for Meditation." Kenzi was way too cheerful as she pulled into an empty parking spot. I took one last drag on the coffee I'd snagged from the Kappa Mu kitchen. Then I set the cup in its holder and followed Brigga out of the car.

"Just look at that ocean." Kenzi beamed as she closed the door behind her. "Isn't it a glorious morning?"

"It's beautiful." Janna climbed gracefully from the front seat. "Ingrid, you okay?"

"Yeah." I rubbed my eyes. "Sorry, I don't know why I'm so tired today."

"I do," Brigga said slyly. "You didn't come home until well after midnight. Good thing we have an extended weekend curfew."

"The bus brought us back at ten-thirty." Kenzi tilted her face to the sun. "Did you guys go out after the beach?"

"Ingrid and Axel took a 'walk.'" Brigga made quotes in the air with her fingers.

"We *did* walk," I objected.

"Mmm-hmm." Janna arched one brow.

"We did." I tugged the hem of my tank top lower around my hips.

"And is that *all* you did?" Brigga pressed.

"Well . . ."

"Good for you." Kenzi laughed. "Axel's hot. And he has good chi. Your energies complement one another beautifully."

"Uh . . . thanks?"

"Don't thank me." Kenzi waved her hand. "It's a fact. Just like it's a fact that this retreat is going to blow your minds. Torstein is *the best*. He's the most grounded soul I've ever encountered. And his meditations are beyond inspiring. You're going to come away from today with a whole new perspective on your human life."

My eyes met Janna's, and we shrugged. We'd learned not to react when Kenzi started talking about soul lives, and energy, and juju. If we asked questions, we only ended up more confused.

"Okay." Janna clapped her hands together. "So . . . which way is the entrance?"

"It's up here." Kenzi walked around the front of the car and turned toward a grassy slope. I followed along the low embankment, shielding my eyes as the sun bounced off the sea from my left. The water was smooth, its glassy surface shifting subtly in the slight breeze. Despite my exhaustion, I couldn't help but appreciate the stillness. It reminded me of the ocean's calm during my early morning workouts in the shieldmaiden compound. Janna and I took regular sunrise climbs along the Cliffs of Conquest. At that hour, the ocean could be the absolute picture of peace.

"Whoa. Is that it?" Brigga's awed tone made me look up. "It's huge."

The massive glass structure was certainly that. The building was only two stories tall, but it was easily half the width of Valkyris' castle. And it stretched far enough into the distance that I guessed it be nearly as long, too.

Was this whole thing just for meditating?

"That's only the south campus." Kenzi gestured ahead. "Beyond this building, there's a pool and then a group of single-story structures that are more intimate. The crystal room is on the north campus, and we do more intimate healings in that space."

I eyed the two-story enclosure in front of me. "And this space is for . . ."

"Meditation rooms face the ocean. Library is in the

back. The rest of the rooms are admin, reiki rooms, film studios—"

"Film studios?" Janna tilted her head.

"Torstein runs an empire," Kenzi said proudly. "His teachings are really *avant-garde*, and tons of people want to study with him. But there's only so much space at the center, so he films recordings of some of his more impactful meditations. He makes some of them free through his website in order to help as many souls as possible awaken to their true purpose. And he sells the more advanced meditations for those who want to accelerate their ascension."

Very little of that made sense to me, so I stifled my yawn and nodded. "Right."

"We'd better get inside if we want to get spots up front." Kenzi waved us forward. "Come on."

We walked toward the entrance, and gave our names to the white-clad woman at the desk.

"The morning session is in the enclave." The woman smiled serenely at Kenzi. "You know where you're going."

"I do. Namaste, Meredith." Kenzi folded her hands and bowed.

"Namaste." Meredith mirrored Kenzi's motion. Janna, Brigga, and I murmured soft *Namastes* before following our friend through the compound.

"This place feels weird," I whispered to Janna. "It's too . . . white."

"There does seem to be a definite color scheme," Janna agreed.

"Maybe they spent all their money on the windows and didn't have anything left over for paint?" I blinked as we passed a sitting area lined with four white couches, a white table, and a tea-service tray filled with white mugs.

"I think it's a choice." Janna tilted her chin at the white-clad staff member standing behind the tea setup. "Maybe it inspires serenity."

"Our Seers back home wear loads of color," I pointed out. "And crystals."

Gods, they wore so many crystals. Necklaces, earrings, bracelets, *toe rings* . . .

"Things have evolved, I suppose." Janna shrugged. "Try to keep an open mind. You never know, we might end up learning something."

"Unless we're going to learn how to stop our mage from disappearing come capture time, this seems like an exercise in futility."

"No exercise is ever futile," Janna said. "Besides, our target won't be making his move for another week and a half. What else are we going to do?"

I could think of a lot of things I'd have rather been doing right then. But we'd just reached the end of the long hallway, and Kenzi turned to beam at us with her easy smile. She opened the door and held it open. We filed through one by one, until we all stood in a tranquil, outdoor space.

"Whoa." I spun a slow circle, taking in the scene. The courtyard was framed by ivory columns, each draped in greens that climbed from low pots up their mottled, white surfaces to lace through the trellises that shaded the grass below. A fountain bubbled in one corner, while fragrant blooms lined either side of the lawn. The scene was one of absolute peace. Maybe the gods had crafted it on a visit to modern-day Midgard.

The gods . . . or the guru.

Torstein emerged from the far end of the courtyard —a vision of serenity in his sleeveless, white shirt and loose-fitting pants. His melodic voice floated across the calm as he stretched his arms out to his sides. "*Velkommen*, my friends. It's wonderful to see each of you."

"Namaste, Torstein." Kenzi folded her hands together.

"Namaste, my sister of the light." Torstein bowed, and Kenzi did the same. "And Ingrid. Brigga. Janna." Torstein bowed to each of us in turn. "What a blessing to be joined by such bright spirits on this beautiful November morning."

"Thanks for having us," Brigga bubbled. "You have a really beautiful facility."

"We have been more than blessed," Torstein agreed. "I'd be happy to show you around after the morning session. We'll be facing the sea today—channeling Njord's tranquility and fortitude."

I'd grown up in a fishing village, so I knew all about Njord. But for someone on this landmass . . . in this time . . .

"Njord, the Norse sea god?" I blinked at Torstein. "Are you . . . do you believe in . . ."

How did I ask Torstein if he worshipped our gods, when he lived in an era where people thought Thor was just a character in a comic book?

"I believe in light," Torstein said. "In the greater good of the human spirt. And in *all* of the deities that have guided mankind throughout the ages."

Right. Obviously. Because Torstein may have spent a decade alone in a Norwegian forest, but he was still from this century. And worshipping gods who were already falling from fashion in our own time was no way to run a meditation empire.

"Torstein is open to *all* paths which lead us to our highest self," Kenzi said. "And speaking of, my highest self needs to hydrate. I'll grab waters for you guys, too."

"I'll help you," Janna offered. She followed Kenzi to an ice-laden bin near one of the columns.

"I'll get us spots up front. You said you'll be right there?" Brigga pointed to the row of meditation mats nearest the cliff's edge.

"I'll be leading from the ocean side, *ja*." Torstein turned his focus to me as Brigga scampered to claim our mats. "Ingrid."

"Torstein," I said lightly. Now that I was alone with him, that weird tingling had returned to my spine.

"I am most pleased that you were able to join me today." Torstein held out his hands and turned his palms upward. "May I?"

"Uh . . . sure?" I placed my hands in his, ignoring the buzz that built along my skin. When Torstein closed his eyes, I jumped at the surge that shot up my arm. I quickly pulled my hands away, rubbing them together as I stepped back. "I'd better, uh, get settled. Up there. With Brigga."

"Of course." Torstein's long, blond hair fell over his shoulders as he bowed. "Namaste, sister Ingrid."

"Yes. Right." I backed slowly away, ignoring the sparks shooting up and down my spine. That was the second time in as many days I'd had a physical reaction to a total stranger. Why did Kenzi's guru have this effect on me?

And why the Helheim was he looking at me like I was the answer to some long-awaited question?

CHAPTER 8

"THAT WAS EXCELLENT WORK this morning, my brothers and sisters of the light." Torstein stood at the edge of the lawn, the ocean reflecting brilliant sunbeams at his golden halo of hair. His loose, white pants fluttered in the soft breeze as he pressed his hands together and bent low at the waist. "Namaste."

I untangled my limbs from their current pretzel-like position as the chorus of yogis behind me chanted, "Namaste."

"As always, lunch will be served in the outdoor atrium. You're welcome to remain there or take your food to a more solitary location should you wish to remain in meditation. Our souls will reconvene in one hour's time—Meredith will sound the gong as a gentle reminder." Torstein stretched his arms in an arc over his head. He joined his hands in prayer as he brought them to his chest and closed his eyes. It was impossible not to notice the way his triceps popped with the motion. Or the way his lightly tanned skin glinted beneath the sun.

Not that I was looking.

"Go in peace, my fellow cosmic travelers." Torstein opened his eyes, scanning the lawn with his signature look—the one that straddled serenity and intensity. The guru was the physical embodiment of inner peace, and yet . . . there was definitely a secondary motivation bubbling beneath that calculated level of calm.

And when his sky-blue stare settled intently on me, I had couldn't help but wonder just what it was.

"So?" Torstein strode confidently in the direction of my yoga mat. "How did you find this morning's session?"

"It was *wonderful.*" Brigga spoke breathily from beside me. "I feel so connected to my inner goddess."

Janna leaned forward to shoot me a *look*—one that clearly said, "Here we go again."

"I agree." Kenzi spoke up from my left. "The empowerment affirmations really resonated. I feel like my vibration ascended to a whole new level."

"It has," Torstein confirmed. "You did wonderful work today, Kenzi."

Kenzi's cheeks absolutely glowed. "Thank you."

"Thank *you* for putting in the effort to elevate the planetary consciousness. When one soul ascends, we all rise in the collective light." Torstein spoke without so much as a hint of irony.

Sure . . .

"Ingrid." Torstein angled his shoulders toward me and folded his hands together at his waist.

"Torstein." There it was—that bizarre tingling that shot up and down my back whenever he focused on me. I squirmed uncomfortably under his stare.

"I wondered if you might be willing to join me on a walk around the grounds. Your energy is particularly . . . metamorphic today, and I believe I have something that might be of assistance in your ascension journey."

A frustrated *harrumph* came from my right.

"I . . . uh . . ." I tore my gaze from the blue beams of intensity and blinked at Janna. Shieldmaiden protocol dictated that we rarely move alone in the field. Since we were technically on a mission, I wanted my captain to weigh in on why it was a bad idea to go off alone with the attractive, chiseled guru.

Or maybe I wanted her permission.

"I'm certain you're hungry, so I won't keep you long," Torstein said easily. "You'll be able to join your friends for lunch while I pave the golden path of intention for our afternoon session."

What the Helheim is a golden path of intention?

"Go on, Ingrid," Kenzi said excitedly. "Torstein *rarely* offers a one-on-one. You must be on the verge of a huge breakthrough."

"We'll grab you a plate," Janna confirmed. My heart leapt at her slight nod.

"Okay then." I pushed myself to my feet, cringing at the slight pull in my hamstring. I was a shieldmaiden, for Frigga's sake. How did a morning of *stretching* hurt this much?

"Wonderful." Torstein offered me his arm, and I hesitated. "Touch helps me to read your vibration," he said quietly.

From the ground, Kenzi shot me a thumbs-up.

"Oh. Right. Well, uh, see you, guys." I offered a half-hearted wave before resting my palm on Torstein's forearm. The now familiar spark shot through my hand, sending a jolt to my heart.

"See you at lunch," Janna said, at the same time Brigga muttered, "Lucky."

Torstein placed his hand atop mine and guided us away from the group. We walked in silence, the soft grass tickling my bare feet. The guru stared out at the ocean as we moved, and I couldn't stop myself from sneaking occasional glances at his profile. His hair hung loose around thick, bronzed shoulders. His clear blue eyes stared unblinkingly at the crystalline sea. He held himself with an air of calm, and strength, and absolute authority.

No wonder he'd amassed a legion of followers.

When we reached the end of the glass building, we paused in front of a massive pool. A handful of people swam slow laps along its length, while others sat cross-legged in shaded domes scattered across its perimeter. We skirted around an outdoor yoga class, then made our way toward what must have been the north compound—a cluster of single-story buildings that looked like they would have been more at home in a fairy tale than along the cliffs of Malibu. They were simple cottages complete with low shrubs and bursting blooms—white ones, of course—that lined the walkways that connected them. Torstein approached one, slowing his steps as he shifted to face me.

"You're wondering why I've brought you here." He slipped my hand off his arm, and clasped it between his own.

"Um . . . to . . . uh, something about ascension? Or soul acceleration?" Or whatever the morning's class had been about?

"Something like that." Torstein's smile shone with a brilliance that rivaled the sun. "Ingrid, you're an exceptional spirit. Strong. Determined. Incredibly loyal."

"You got all that from my hand?"

"I feel it in your energy. Your vibration is remarkably similar to mine. Surely, you can sense that."

What I sensed was that maybe going off alone with the unnervingly attractive guru had been a questionable life choice. "Um . . ." I carefully extracted my hand. "Look, Torstein, I'm really flattered. But I'm with Axel, and—"

"Ah. The warrior."

My pulse stilled. *How does he know that?* "What did you say?"

"Axel has a warrior's spirit," Torstein said. The vise on my chest loosened. "He was ready to take me down last night on the pier. He is overprotective of you, yes?"

"He's cautious," I conceded. "With *everyone*."

"I see." Torstein rubbed his jaw. "And while caution

is prudent, one must always be open to the unique circumstances presented by the universe. Don't you agree?"

I shifted my weight. "So, what did you want to talk to me about?"

One corner of Torstein's mouth drew upward. "You're direct. I appreciate that."

"Well?"

Torstein glanced toward the complex. "I think it would be better to show you instead."

"Okay."

He walked toward the building nearest the ocean without saying a word. Not knowing what else to do, I followed. When he reached the door, he raised his palm to a small box along its edge. An orb emerged from the wall on the right, and Torstein leaned in so his eye was level with its surface. "Retinal scan," he said by way of explanation.

What the Helheim?

The door clicked open. Torstein held out his hand. "After you."

My shoulder blades pulled reflexively downward, and the cool metal of my twin daggers pressed against my skin. I'd strapped both my fighting dagger and Freia's magical blade to my spine—one to wield, the other to protect. I was armed. I was a shieldmaiden. I could take Torstein if it came to that.

Relax, Ingrid. He's just some new-aged guru, remember?
But those arms are pretty massive . . .
Stop looking at Torstein's arms.

Right.

I stepped over the threshold. Inside, the cottage was dark. Since the windows were firmly shuttered, I couldn't see Torstein when he walked in behind me. My arms tensed as the door clicked closed and I realized how isolated we really were.

Just a guru, remember?

"Sorry about the darkness. Let me. . ." Torstein's arm brushed against mine as he reached for what must have been the lights. Heat jolted along my skin as he pulled away, and the room was illuminated in a faint, golden glow. The cottage was sparsely furnished—a small sitting area framed the wall with the fireplace, while a little kitchen nestled in the opposite corner. In the center stood what appeared to be a sculpture—an obelisk with familiar etchings marking the upper two thirds.

I walked toward the structure, curiosity trumping caution. "Are those . . . runes?"

"Indeed." Torstein stayed by the door.

I ran my fingertips along the symbols. "I haven't seen anything like this here. Why are there runes in the middle of Los Angeles?"

"We're in Malibu." Torstein chuckled. "And Norway is my country, too."

My hand froze atop a symbol that looked like an arrow—the rune for *Tyr*, the Norse God of War. The very one my people channeled in battle. "I never said I was from Norway."

"Kenzi did when she introduced us," Torstein

reminded me.

"Oh."

Stop being so paranoid.

"Why don't you rest your palm against that one?" Torstein nodded at my hand. "You seem to have an affinity for it."

Uh . . . okay.

I stretched my hand across Tyr's rune, and a flash of heat coursed along my skin. As the burn swept through my palm, I instinctively tried to pull back. But my hand had become one with the obelisk. It melded into the surface, the stone softening as it drew me farther inward. My chest tightened. I wrapped my free hand around my wrist and tugged. The motion only seemed to drag me in more.

"Torstein!" I braced my heels against the ground and wrenched my body backward. "Stop this!"

"This is not my doing." Why the Helheim did he sound so calm?

"If it's not you"—I yanked harder—"then who's making my—*ow!*"

"Stay still, Ingrid," Torstein soothed. "This is a good thing."

"It—*ow!* Doesn't—*ugh.* Feel—*ouch!* Good!" I pulled to my left, then my right. Nothing could sever this excruciating bond.

"It's an affirmation."

I jumped at the voice directly beside my ear. Torstein ran his fingers along my arm, sliding his own palm against the back of my hand so it covered the pulsing flesh. The burn instantly subsided. Torstein withdrew his hand and the obelisk released its hold. I pulled my hand to my chest, rubbing fiercely at the uncomfortable tingling sensation that remained.

What is happening?

Torstein bowed his head as the stone fell slowly to the side. It came to rest on the ground, its base shifting back to reveal a small, circular opening. Inside, stretching deep beneath the floor, lay . . .

"Is that a staircase?" I gaped at the secret chamber underneath the cottage. "Torstein, I swear to Odin, if you don't tell me what's happening right this minute, I will—"

"Patience, Ingrid." Torstein placed his palms on either side of my arms.

My shoulder blades twitched reflexively around my daggers.

"I will explain everything. Once we're safely inside."

"If you think I'm following you into a hole in the ground after *that*, then you're clearly delusional."

"Maybe." He squeezed my shoulders lightly. "But I think you're going to want to see what's down there."

I stepped out of his hold. "Give me one good reason I should trust you."

"Because your hand is perfectly fine. Look." Torstein waited as I examined my still-tingling flesh. Sure enough, it bore no burn marks—the skin wasn't even warm. It was as if nothing had happened.

Am I going crazy?

"What you felt was purely illusory," Torstein

explained. "That particular rune reads energy—it's coded to grant entry to only those souls whose vibration aligns with my own. As it reads, it emits a resonance that mimics the body's reaction to heat. Your hand was never actually burning—the rune just sent those signals to your brain's processing sensors."

"What. The. Helheim?"

"Don't you believe in science?"

My eyes narrowed. "What I don't believe in is *you*. What kind of game are you playing here, *guru*?"

"There's something I need you to see." Torstein stepped onto the staircase. "The runes don't lie, Ingrid. I can trust you."

"Lucky me."

"Please?" Torstein's eyes met mine. He stared me down, his signature intensity deepening his gaze. Whatever lay at the bottom of those stairs, it was obvious that he *really* wanted me to see it.

The question was, *should I*?

CHAPTER 9

DESPITE MY HESITATION, I reluctantly followed Torstein. Fake-heat-inducing column aside, it was clear there was more to the guru than meditative mastery. If he was hiding something in this secret chamber, I wanted to know what it was.

How I'd get that knowledge above ground remained to be seen.

The staircase spiraled into a stone hallway. Glowing sconces lined each wall, lending a slight illumination to the passage. Torstein moved seamlessly toward a wooden door—one lined with iron bars that scrolled in intricate patterns not unlike those at Valkyris Academy. As we moved along the hall, I raised one hand to my shoulder. I needed to be ready to rip my fighting dagger from its sheath if things took a turn. But when Torstein placed his hand on the wall panel, the door clicked quietly open. No monsters emerged; no hand-searing runes flew forward. Torstein simply pushed on the door and stepped into a faint, blue glow. The space emitted a soft hum—one not unlike the sound of the singing bowls Torstein had used during the morning's meditation. My curiosity thoroughly piqued, I moved toward the light.

Please, Odin, don't let me regret this.

"It's okay, Ingrid. I'm not going to hurt you."

Said every perpetrator ever before initiating an attack.

"I'm not a perpetrator," Torstein sighed.

Did I say that out loud?

"You didn't have to," Torstein said. "The crystals enhance the *clairs*—clairaudience, clairsentience, clairvoyance . . ."

"Claire who?" I stepped through the doorway and into a small room. A cluster of blue-white crystals perched atop a glass table. Each gem was easily a foot tall, with roughly six flat sides peaking at one pointed end. The bottom edges were flat, allowing the crystals to stand upright so they formed a circle at the table's center. They pinged both light and sound between them, creating a harmonious, glowing orb that encompassed the entire space.

"Holy Mother Frigga. What are those?"

"Quanta crystals." Torstein stared at the orb. "When they're together, they form a protection—an impenetrable sphere. They reject foreign objects from their sacred space, excepting those whose vibrations align with their divine purpose."

I really wished Torstein spoke in plain English. The magical inner-ear translator activated by the time-traveling dagger we'd used to jump here could only get me so far. "Smaller words, *guru*."

"You and I can touch the stones because our energies are aligned with theirs. We're on the side of the light—not the darkness."

I still had no idea what he was talking about. If this was some weird way of flirting with me, he had—

Wait. Did he say . . .

"Did you call them quanta crystals?" My hand crept toward my back.

"I did."

Dritt.

"Quanta crystals." I reached behind me until my fingertips brushed the hilt of my dagger. "As in, crystals infused with cosmic energy?"

"Yes." The flickering light illuminated Torstein's too-intense stare.

"The same crystals that are alleged to be imbued with magic thanks to an astronomical alignment and a charged beam of light?" I'd heard this story in Astronomy. My teacher had written these particular crystals off as a myth, while my classmates wanted to use them to finance their dream homes and student films. But the truth was . . .

Oh, gods.

"Again, yes."

My pulse stilled. If Torstein was who I thought he

was, then I'd jeopardized everything we'd come here to protect.

I had to get out of there.

I checked that Freia's dagger was secure against my spine before wrapping my palm around the hilt of my fighting blade. "Are these crystals, by any chance, ingredients one might use for, say, a spell?"

"One to *Control Mankind And All The Realms*?" Torstein's eyes narrowed.

Double dritt.

My brain clicked into combat mode. Without another word, I yanked my dagger from its sheath and charged toward Torstein. My blade nicked the side of his forearm as he leapt from my path.

"Ingrid! What are you—"

"You're working with him?" I shifted my weight to deliver a fierce kick to Torstein's chest. He stumbled backward, his shoulders slamming into the wall.

"No!" Torstein raised his hands, but I pivoted onto one foot, stalling his attack with a strong roundhouse. The slap of my bare heel on his arms echoed around the room, creating an eerie dissonance with the still-singing crystals. As Torstein righted himself, I swung my dagger-arm and jammed the blade into his thigh. He cringed, but didn't make a sound as he wrapped one hand around mine and ripped the weapon from his leg. "Ingrid. Stop this."

"That's why you brought me here?"

My left fist flew toward his jaw. He easily blocked the blow.

"You're collecting the ingredients for his spell, and you want—"

Do not let him get Freia's dagger. Do not.

"What I want is—arugh." Torstein winced as I pulled my hand free of his grasp and slammed it back down. My blade pierced his thigh a second time. His hair fell in front of his face as he folded forward. He removed the blade and flung it across the room before lifting his head to meet my steely stare. "I wouldn't do that again."

"I'm not afraid of you." I shuffled backward, toward the crystals. If he thought I was leaving them with him, he wasn't as bright as his peace-loving followers believed.

"Well, maybe you should be." Torstein raised one hand and held it at chest level. When I reached for the crystals, he sent a beam of light from his palm. It struck my hand with a white-hot heat.

I swore loudly, shaking off the burn.

"I just want to talk to you." *Said the crazy man shooting hand beams.* "I'm not crazy, Ingrid."

"How are you reading my—never mind." I flung myself at the crystals, intending to tackle them to the ground. But no sooner had I leapt for their table than another beam shot from Torstein's palm. This one struck me in the chest, knocking the breath from my lungs and suspending me midair. My legs kicked as I struggled to break free, but it was no use. I was trapped. The dark mage's minion had me strung up—

immobilized, incapacitated, and completely and totally incapable of fighting him off.

Think, Ingrid. What would Axel do?

Axel would kill me for getting myself into this situation. Of that, I was certain.

"I won't let you do this," I swore. I wrenched my shoulders from side to side, fighting against Torstein's hold. With each twist, a fresh burn erupted across my chest. *Gods!* "Whatever you throw at me—whatever black magic you possess—you're going to have to fight me to the death. Because, Odin as my witness, I will *never—augh!*"

"I just want you to *listen* to me."

"Put me down or so help me I'll make sure you rot in Hel—"

"Enough! I'm one of you. Can't you see that?" Torstein raised his hands, and I dropped to the ground with a thud. Pain shot across my back, and I arched my spine to shift the guard of Freia's blade from the crater it now carved into my skin.

"Augh." I rolled to one side and struggled to push myself up. I dug my fingertips into the floor as the fire across my chest raged anew. How did I make this stop?

"I'm not with the dark mage—I've spent the past six hundred years fighting *against* him. We're on the same team, Ingrid."

"I don't believe you." I spoke through gritted teeth, rubbing my still-burning flesh. "Only a mage could do that kind of magic."

"Correct." Torstein spoke urgently. "Only a mage *can* do true magic. But not all mages are dark."

My breath hitched. "Wait. Are you saying . . ."

"I'm a light mage, Ingrid. The one who created the quanta crystals and scattered them across the realms. And I want to join your fight."

CHAPTER 10

S EVEN WORDS. WITH SEVEN little words, Torstein had changed everything.

"What do you mean, you want to join our fight?"

"We have to stop Sverrir."

"Who?"

"The dark mage," Torstein explained. "If he acquires the materials he needs to complete his spell, he'll use it to destroy this world . . . and rebuild one based in chaos."

"I know that." My breath shuddered as a residual heat wave coursed through me. I brought both hands to my collarbone. "But how do *you*—arugh."

"Let me help." Torstein stepped closer. "May I?"

I eyed him warily. "Are you going to burn me? Or string me up the air?"

"I apologize. I was protecting the crystals. So long as you pose no threat to them, it won't happen again."

"It better not," I muttered. With great reluctance, I

allowed Torstein to place his palm across my sternum. He closed his eyes and murmured something I couldn't quite make out. But the moment the words passed his lips, relief arrived. The burning dissipated, seemingly absorbed by his touch. In its place, my skin was left with a pleasant tingle—one made only slightly awkward by the fact that Torstein's hand was just inches away from my breasts. "Ahem."

Torstein's eyes blinked open. Piercing blue orbs bored straight through me, their intensity making me shift where I sat.

"You are still uncomfortable," he deduced.

"You're almost touching my . . ." I jutted my chin downward.

"Of course." Torstein withdrew his hand, then knelt on the ground beside me. "Does anything else hurt?"

My spine ached. One knee throbbed from where I'd cracked it on the hard floor. And a dull pounding in the back of my head let me know it was strongly considering exploding. But I didn't want to give Axel another reason to kill Torstein, so I just shrugged. "I'm fine."

"I can heal you remotely if you're worried about Axel."

"How do you know what I was—"

"Shh." Torstein raised his hand. A pale-pink mist immediately swept forward. I tried not to panic as it coursed over me, cloaking me in a light layer of pressure.

"Are you sure this is—"

"One more moment." Torstein raised and lowered

his hand before pulling his fingers into his palm. The mist slowly retracted, taking with it every drop of my residual pain. "That should be better."

A quick scan of my injuries confirmed his diagnosis. *How did he do that?* "Uh, thanks?"

"I apologize for hurting you." Torstein retrieved my dagger from the corner of the room and placed it on the ground beside me. "And I am sorry for the secrecy. These crystals are very important to me. They must be protected. Because the last time Sverrir went after them, he . . ."

Torstein's face fell, a mask of despair marring his serenity.

"Why don't you tell me how you got involved in all of this?" I picked up my dagger and rested it across my lap. *Just in case.*

"Of course." Torstein held his palm over his thigh. The pink mist immediately set to work healing the stab wounds I'd inflicted.

Not sorry.

"I come from a long line of light magic wielders," Torstein began. "Mages, as we came to be known. For generations, my family stood alongside fellow warriors of the light. We fought to protect this world from the dark forces who wished to overtake it. Fire giants and frost giants, demons and wraiths. And of course, the dark mages those creatures use as vessels here on Earth."

My fingertips brushed the guard of my dagger. "Go on."

"I was fairly young during the original planetary alignment—the one that occurred during the Viking Age. I was not yet advanced enough to understand its significance. And I was still hiding my powers then—magic wielders were not looked kindly upon during that time."

Didn't I know it . . .

"But as the years went on, other mages passed down stories of the artifacts created during that alignment—of their ability to perform miracles and to generate life. These were the kinds of objects men had gone to war in order to possess. When we realized a second alignment was coming, we feared the power it could create. A surge that funneled through so many planets was bound to imbue whatever it touched with unparalleled cosmic strength. If it activated a light object, its properties would be enhanced for the greatest good of all. But if it activated a dark one . . ."

"Let me guess. Chaos?"

"Precisely." Torstein brushed an errant stand of hair from his face. "And so, the mages of the Council of Light convened in northern Norway. We mapped out the exact point of impact and traveled to it. And we brought along the most powerful crystal in our possession."

"The quanta crystals?" I guessed.

"Crystal," Torstein corrected. "Singular. Back then, it was one pure formation, forged in the heart of an Icelandic volcano and carried by dolphins to the shores of Lapland. For hundreds of years it was protected by indigenous tribes. But shortly before the second align-ment, they turned it over to the Council of Light. Their elders sensed a threat, and they knew we were the crystal's best chance at survival."

I drew my knees to my chest. "Continue."

"When the planets aligned, we set the crystal in a sacred grove, formed our protective circle, and waited. The surge came just as predicted—devastatingly strong and immensely powerful. Its reverberations killed two of our council, while a third went mad—he touched the crystal before the power had time to settle. Those of us who remained knew we had to protect the quanta. Our war with the dark mages had already begun, and we had a dragon waiting nearby to carry the crystal to a cave in the far north. But when we signaled, our trans-port didn't come. Our enemies had found us. And they'd massacred our most sacred creature."

Torstein's head bowed. "My memories of the battle are blurred. Most of my brethren were killed. The dark mages had the high ground—along with the element of surprise. Ama and I were the only survivors. We managed to drag the crystal to a nearby cove. But the dark mages were tracking us, and we knew the only way to protect the stone was to divide it. Ama broke it into a dozen pieces, and we each took six to scatter across the world. I hid mine among the Northern Territories, while Ama took hers to what was then uncharted land here in the west. We were supposed to meet in Iceland—to build our life together once the crystals were safely hidden. But

Ama never came. Sverrir had followed her west. And he'd . . ."

Pain haunted Torstein's face. Agony danced across his eyes, and I couldn't help but reach out to rest my hand on his arm. "I'm so sorry, Torstein."

He merely nodded. "Sverrir abandoned his search for many years. But he's back on his hunt, and he *cannot* to succeed. My twin soul gave her life to stop him. I won't allow that to have been for nothing."

Behind me, the crystals sang louder. I glanced over my shoulder to find them bathed in an even brighter glow. "These crystals here, are they the ones from Europe?"

"*Ja,*" Torstein confirmed. "I collected them after Ama's death. Then I came to search for hers. But Ama was more powerful than I could ever be. She cloaked them so well that I'm still unable to track them. But I understand that to be a great skill of yours. And I'm hoping that together, we'll able to do what I alone could not."

"Do you really think we can find them?"

"I hope to gods that we can. Because if Sverrir gets to even one of them before we do . . ."

My thumb pressed against my dagger. "I've got a lot riding on him *not* enacting that spell too. The place—and the time—that I come from . . . he wants to wipe it from existence."

I bit on my bottom lip, hoping Torstein wouldn't ask me to explain.

He met my gaze with a calm nod. "Then it seems we

have a mutual goal."

Whew.

"I guess we do." The crystals' volume increased again, and a brilliant pulse shot through the room. I raised my hand to my eyes, squinting against the light. "Do you know how to turn them down?"

Torstein chuckled. "They approve of our partnership. They long to be reunited with their other half."

"Uh . . . sure." Because crystals having feelings was totally a thing that made sense.

Snort.

"I understand that much of this is strange to you," Torstein offered. "But many so-called inanimate objects have feelings."

"How are you doing that?" I bristled. "Are you reading my mind?"

"Proximity to the stones enhances my gifts. I can stop if you'd prefer?"

"I would prefer. I would prefer that very much, thank you. If I have something to say, I'll say it to your face."

Torstein tilted his head. "Why don't you try it?"

"I can't read minds." *Obviously.*

"You'll find that you can here. What am I thinking?" Torstein closed his eyes and sat in silence.

Once again, my day had taken a bizarre turn. "Torstein, I don't think—"

"Just *try*, Ingrid."

Sigh.

"Fine. Uh . . . you're hungry? We need to get back

for the afternoon session?"

"Both true, but neither of those was my predominant thought. Try again."

"Look, this is insane. I'm glad we're on the same side here, but—"

"Please." Torstein opened his eyes. "Try again."

"Okay." I sighed. Staring intently at Torstein's forehead, I focused on whatever mysteries were hidden beneath that thick mane of hair. "You're thinking . . . uh . . . oh. Oh! My gods, you've killed people with that crazy hand beam thing."

"Yes." A slow smile spread across Torstein's face. "Well done, Ingrid. I told you that you could do it."

"*Ja*. Well, it's no great victory if I have to see *that*." I shuddered. "Think about something else. Something less disturbing."

"All right. Try again."

I stared at Torstein's brow. After a moment, a low voice filled my head.

. . . and the afternoon session will focus on cleansing the sixth chakra, so we'll need to ensure absolute silence from the western-facing—

"You're going over your meditation." I arched one brow. "This is insane. How did your voice get in my head?"

"Good." Torstein stood and crossed to the table. He removed two of the crystals from their location in the center and held one toward me. "Take this. It will link us into perpetuity."

"Into what?"

"We'll be able to communicate *beyond* the stones' physical presence. Indefinitely."

"Uh, no offense, but I'm not sure I want you in my head all the time." Or ever.

"Our connection will remain at will," Torstein said. "I won't be able to hear your thoughts unless you allow it."

"Even so, that's a really weird—"

"Sverrir is not to be underestimated," Torstein snapped. "Ama was the most powerful light mage I've ever known. If he managed to kill her . . ." Torstein drew a shaky breath.

"Listen, I get that—"

"Our alliance is key to defeating him." Torstein pulled his shoulders back. "Our goals are mutually aligned. And if we do not utilize every advantage we have, we will fail. So, I beg of you. Please. Take the crystal."

I closed my eyes. "You won't hear me unless I want you to?"

"You have my word."

"And you really think this is absolutely necessary?"

"You and I will face Sverrir together. It's inevitable. But he's going to isolate us, and without a means of communication . . . we'll both be destroyed. And our worlds along with us."

Ice raced through my veins. "How can you be sure?"

"Because I've seen it," Torstein said quietly. "I've seen the end of our worlds, Ingrid. And it all starts today."

CHAPTER 11

"WHAT THE HELHEIM, TORSTEIN?"

"Sverrir is about to collect a key item." Torstein frowned. "Darkness has been swirling through this realm all morning. It began shortly after our meditation and has been steadily increasing since."

"Where is he?" I jumped to my feet.

"I don't know." Torstein shook his head. "I only know that he's one step closer to completing his goal. I'm not sure which ingredients he's already collected, or which remain unprocured—besides the quanta crystals, of course. I've made certain he can never get his hands on these."

"But he could get the other six, right? The ones Ama hid are still out there somewhere?"

"Correct." Torstein frowned. "And while he cannot enact the full power of the *Control* spell without all twelve, surely he can create some level of chaos with those we haven't secured."

"Then we have to find them first. And everything else he doesn't have yet." *The crystals, the balboa bark, and the moonstone.* "He's already got meteor rock and illy flower."

"How do you know this?"

"We found his hideout, and apparently he's got a bad memory because he's a list-maker. I'll explain later." I held out my hand. "Give me that crystal. I still don't like the idea, but I'm willing to merge our minds, or whatever you call it. Anything to make sure that monster doesn't destroy our world. Just don't tell Axel I let you in my head, okay?"

"He doesn't like me."

"Most guys don't like tall, attractive men who own castles on the coast and ask to brain-bond to their girl-friends."

A slow grin stretched across Torstein's face. "You find me attractive?"

"Yes. No. I don't know. It doesn't matter." I snatched the crystal from Torstein's hand. "Just don't make my life any harder than it already is. Promise?"

"You have my word." Torstein squared his shoulders so he faced me. "Hold the crystal between your palms— like this."

I did as he instructed, folding my hands against the white-blue rod and lifting it in front of my heart. Torstein muttered words I couldn't understand, and a slow heat filled my torso. It radiated upward, until my head, neck, and shoulders tingled with a vibration so intense, my breath stalled in my chest. "Is. This. N-n-normal?" I chattered.

"Shh." Torstein continued his mumbling, and the tremors slid along my arms. My entire body shook as a white beam burst from Torstein's crystal to mine. A second pulse shot back, and everything stilled. A deep peace settled over me, the chaos of the previous moment now gone.

What. The. Helheim?

Language, Ingrid.

The words inside my head weren't my own. My gods, was that him?

Yes. Torstein smiled. *It worked.*

I thought you said I had to invite you in!

There's no need to shout. And technically, that's true, Torstein agreed. *But your consent was implied at the moment of our merge.*

I glared. *Well, I revoke that consent. Effective* right now.

"Fair enough," Torstein spoke aloud. "I won't return until invited. Just send me a thought—or picture yourself knocking on my head. I am always open to you."

This was going to be beyond weird. But if the future of our worlds depended on it . . .

Gods, I hope Axel's okay with this.

"We should get back to the others." Torstein took the crystal from my hands and placed it back on the table. He did the same with his own, reforming the circle of six. The stones promptly resumed their quiet song. "You surely need to eat, and we don't want to be late for the afternoon session. It's only two hours, so we can figure out our next steps regarding Sverrir when we're finished."

I followed Torstein out of the crystal room. He locked the door with his handprint before leading me up the stairs and out of the cottage.

"Janna, Brigga, and I are meeting with Axel and Raynor when we get back to campus," I said. "You're welcome to join us, I guess. Looks like our team just grew by one. Odin knows Brigga will be happy to work with you."

"She is quite . . . eager. Isn't she?"

"You have no idea." I rolled my eyes. "But if you thought Axel was protective, watch out for Raynor. I'd steer clear if I were you."

"Noted."

Our bare feet made quick strides across the grass. We'd passed the pool and were nearly back to the main building when Torstein raked his hands through his hair. With a slow breath, he rolled his shoulders and tilted his neck to one side. "If you'll excuse me, I need to prepare for my meditation. But should you need anything . . ." Torstein tapped his forehead. "Send me a message."

"Will do," I said lightly. As I walked toward the courtyard where my friends and lunch waited, I tried not to think about how weird it was that a light mage now had permanent access to my mind.

This mission couldn't get any weirder.

Southern California State was cloaked in dusk by the time I showered, changed, and met Torstein at the library parking lot. Axel and Raynor had gone ahead to reserve us a study room, and Janna and Brigga were inside briefing them on our new teammate. All four were hunkered down in a corner room by the time I walked into the second-story study wing, the guru at my side.

The boys were every bit as excited as I'd expected them to be.

"Why the Helheim is he here?" Axel folded his arms across his chest.

Looked like I'd be adding *diplomat* to my list of mission roles.

I plastered a smile across my face. "You all remember Torstein. Torstein, you know Janna and Brigga from the retreat. And you met Axel and Raynor on the pier yesterday."

"*Hei.*" Brigga finished drawing a map on the wall-to-wall whiteboard. She faced Torstein with a grin. "Ingrid told us that you'd be joining our team. I am *so excited.*"

"*Don't go there,*" I mouthed. Torstein nodded serenely.

"About this whole *joining our team?*" Raynor's arms mirrored Axel's. "What exactly does he know?"

"Down, boys." I patted the air, my palms to the ground. "Torstein's one of us. Well, kind of. He's aware

100

of our . . . situation. He wants to stop the dark mage every bit as much as we do, and he's willing to do whatever it takes to make that happen."

Axel's brows quirked. "How does he know about our target?"

"I fought him six hundred years ago," Torstein said quietly. "During the previous alignment. I was there during the war of the mages. My partner and I were the only survivors."

"I'm sorry for your loss." Janna bowed her head. "Your partner, is she—or he . . ."

"She is dead." Torstein spoke matter-of-factly. "Sverrir—the dark mage—killed her after she refused to disclose the location of the crystals she'd hidden throughout this region."

"Poor Torstein." Brigga flitted to his side. She rested her fingertips on his considerable bicep and asked, "Are you okay?"

"It was a long time ago." Torstein clasped her hand. "But thank you for your kindness."

Across the table, Raynor let out a low growl.

"Anyway, Torstein is here because he wants to help us take Sverrir down." I dropped into a seat next to Axel and quickly filled everyone in on the events of that afternoon. Of Torstein's abilities, his history with our target, and how he'd kept his half of the quanta crystals safe in a secret Malibu vault. I left out the part about our weird mind merge—it didn't seem particularly pertinent, and we had more pressing issues to deal with. "The biggest concern at the moment is the fact that our target is apparently closing in on another object. Torstein knows because he has . . . extrasensory abilities."

"The darkness is even stronger in this region than it was in Malibu." Torstein's brows knitted together. "I felt it the moment I arrived at your university."

"*Ja*, about that." Axel and Raynor exchanged a guarded glance. After a pause, Axel leaned over to whisper in my ear. "You're one hundred percent sure we can trust this guy?"

"He's got the motivation. And he knew more about the dark mage than I did," I whispered back. "I didn't exactly go into detail, but he knows we're not from here—or now—and he seemed to understand. The bottom line is that we need him. You saw what happened last time we tried to bring the target in. Having a light mage on our side could be a game changer. And if he somehow double-crosses us, well . . . it's five on one. Right?"

"I guess . . ." Axel rubbed his neck. His eyes narrowed and he stared silently at Torstein. After a seemingly endless beat, he leaned forward on his elbows and addressed the group. "Raynor and I just got a tip from one of our housemates. It seems the moonstone exhibit is coming in sooner than we expected."

"What? Why?" Janna asked.

"Apparently, the last museum that housed it had to shut the whole thing down a few days early. Some weird tremors rocked their town yesterday, and they closed for structural damage. With the stones no longer on display, the curators decided to send them on to their next stop."

"What exactly does that mean?" Torstein turned to me.

"Our target's looking to acquire three more objects before he can complete the *Control* spell—balboa bark, quanta crystals, and moonstone." He was also after Freia's dagger, but despite my assertions to Axel, I wasn't ready to trust Torstein with that particular information. As far as I was concerned, the fewer people who knew about the dagger's existence—or the fact that I currently wore it strapped to my back—the better. "We think Sverrir is going to go after one of the moonstones coming to the campus museum—the Orb of Máni."

"Why that particular item?" Torstein asked.

"It's supposed to be one of the best-preserved samples of moonstone ever found," I said.

"Plus it's *enormous*," Brigga added. "For a crystal, anyway. It weighs more than thirty pounds."

Torstein let out a low whistle. "That is a sizeable moonstone."

"Our source said that with the arrival change, the exhibit should be ready for viewing by Tuesday evening," Axel continued. "And since it's over a full day's setup—"

"The moonstones must be on the move," Janna deduced. "When will they arrive here?"

Axel checked the clock on the wall. "In about four hours—six if traffic's bad."

"When isn't traffic bad?" I muttered.

"What's our plan?" Torstein asked.

Axel pushed his chair back. He stalked to the white-board and pointed at Brigga's drawing. "Our house-mate works at the museum. According to him, exhibits usually arrive at the loading dock on the west side of the building. The trucks pull right into the bay, so once they reach that spot, exposure will be at a minimum. Now, the closest freeway access is here." Axel tapped the board. "Which, in all likelihood, means the driver will exit there, and take the six-lane road straight to campus. If that happens, he'll be on surface roads for about three minutes before he gets to the dock."

"When will the stones be the least secure?" Janna asked.

"That would be during off-loading," Axel said. "There's a twenty-foot gap between the loading bay and the muse-um's rear entrance. It's covered, but it's the only location in which the objects will be outside of both the truck and the museum. We anticipate some level of confusion during the materials' transfer—as we understand it, multiple workers will assist in unloading the crates."

"It would be pretty easy for even a non-magic wielder to slip in and pretend to be one of the staff," Raynor added.

"So, you're thinking our target will strike then." I blinked at the board. "Where are our stakeout points?"

"Here, here, and here." Axel tapped a triangle around the loading dock. "There are lookout areas on the third and fifth stories of the bell tower. Raynor and Brigga will hide there and use lights to signal us when the target arrives. Janna, I want you at location one." Axel pointed to an *X* along what seemed to be a shrub-lined path. "You're our deadliest fighter, and this is his most likely point of entry. You'll be our front line, but I know you can handle it."

"I'm honored." Janna spoke without so much as a hit of irony.

"Ingrid, I want you here." Axel touched a second *X*. "It's the closest location to the dock, so if he somehow gets past Janna, you'll have access before he reaches the truck. Do whatever it takes to bring him down—use lethal force if necessary."

"With pleasure." I nodded.

One corner of his mouth drew upward. He turned away from me to tap the third *X*. "And I'll be in here."

"How are you going to get inside the museum?" Janna asked.

"Our housemate said they always need extra hands for these kinds of things," Axel said. "I told him I was looking to make a little money, and he got me the job. I report in two hours."

"Excellent." Janna eyed the still-standing light mage. "What about Torstein? We didn't account for a magical assist. Where will you have the best vantage point to do . . . whatever it is you do?"

"I can cast from anywhere." Torstein studied the board. "But if you want me close, I'll position myself somewhere near Ingrid. It looks like she'll have the most cover."

"You sure?" Axel touched a square on the board. "The fountain is pretty big. You may be able to hide out there."

Torstein held Axel's cool stare. "I'll assess my most advantageous location once we're on the ground. Sound good?"

Axel just grunted.

"Seems like we'll have all angles situated," Janna said lightly.

"Unless Sverrir makes his move somewhere along the travel route." Torstein crossed to the whiteboard.

Axel's shoulders tensed. "We've run multiple scenarios, and that particular outcome has been determined to be highly unlikely."

"Perhaps." Torstein folded his arms as he studied at the map. "But I know that this intersection has a long traffic light—it's a full two-minute stop during high travel periods. Sverrir will know that the loading dock should have heightened security. He's more likely to gain easy access *before* the crystals are under observation."

"You're assuming the transport catches the stoplight." Axel shook his head. "We ran that data as well. There's only a twenty percent chance of that happening. Our resources are better spent surrounding the dock."

He and Torstein stared at each other in silence. Tension pinged between them—tiny daggers firing like arrows between their narrowed arms. Finally, Torstein shrugged and crossed to an empty chair. "It's your mission."

Curiosity flickered in my head. Had he really given up that easily?

Biting on my bottom lip, I blinked at my hands and took a risk.

Torstein? I sent the thought into the air.

A light rapping echoed across my forehead.

What the Helheim?

You have to let me in. Torstein's voice filled my head.

What?

I told you I wouldn't violate your privacy, he reiterated. *You have to invite me in.*

Fine. Come in.

Thank you. He sounded pleased.

Gods, this was weird.

Why'd you back down? I asked. *If you really think Sverrir is going to strike at the light . . .*

I can monitor the location remotely, Torstein said. *If I see anything out of the ordinary, I can port myself to a more advantageous location. And bring you with me, if need be.*

My jaw hit my chest. *You can do that?*

It's not hard.

"Ingrid? You okay?" Axel's voice pulled me back to the table.

"Huh? *Ja.* Why?"

"You look . . ." Axel's brow was furrowed. "Concerned."

"Just, uh, mentally running through the mission."

With the voice inside my head. *Snort.* "Sounds like we've got a solid plan."

"I sure hope so." Axel stared at the board. "Odin willing, this thing goes off without issue. We could be on our way home by morning."

Gods, I wished . . .

"What will you do with him?" Torstein asked quietly. "Is Sverrir to be tried or executed?"

A long pause followed his words.

"We're not sure." Janna finally spoke. "Our orders were just to bring him in . . ."

"Mmm." Torstein clasped his hands together. "If lethal force *isn't* used, I should like to have a word with him before you depart. We have some unfinished business between us."

"Of course." Janna nodded.

"Thank you." Torstein cast his gaze downward. No doubt he was thinking of all he'd lost . . . of the family and the future Sverrir had cost him.

Poor thing.

"Okay." Axel's clap broke my lament. "We've got a few hours to prepare, so everybody head back to the houses and suit up for combat. We'll need every tool at our disposal. Grab the swords, daggers, shields—"

"You're going to carry those in the open?" Torstein asked. "There are weapons restrictions in Los Angeles."

"We did it once before," I said. "Everyone thought we were part of a theatre group."

"Ah." Torstein nodded. "Carry on."

"We'll meet in front of the Kappa house in one

hour." Axel stared at each of us in turn. "Be careful tonight. We've seen what we're up against. Keep your guard, and remember what we're fighting for."

"For home," Brigga said wistfully.

"For family." Raynor met Brigga's eyes.

"For valor." Janna placed her fist over her heart.

"For Valkyris," I added.

Axel crossed to my side. He stared at me as he said, "For our future."

My heart tugged as I reached out to take his hand. Absolutely everything was riding on this mission. If we somehow managed to pull this off . . .

I closed my eyes and sent out a silent prayer.

Please, gods, don't let us mess it up.

CHAPTER 12

THE SETUP WENT OFF without a hitch. By eight-thirty that night, Axel, Janna, and I had taken our places around the loading dock. Janna was hidden behind a cluster of columns in front of the student center, while Axel was situated safely inside the museum. I'd tucked myself behind a recently renovated statue, and Brigga and Raynor were obscured from view on the third and fifth floors of the bell tower. Meanwhile, Torstein was . . .

Well, Torstein was pretty much everywhere.

He'd rejected Axel's offered location and had opted instead to work out of a tree, of all places. He claimed it gave him a solid vantage point, while allowing for quick access should his physical presence be required. I couldn't see him anywhere, but I knew he was nearby. And he was always a thought away . . . as he frequently reminded me.

What? I bristled at the third rap across my forehead. This mode of communication was beyond weird.

No sign of the truck on the freeway, he reported. *I'm not picking up any moonstone signatures either.*

I'll let the others know.

I signaled Axel with one of the lights he'd snagged from his housemate. He, Janna, and I wore them strapped to our heads, while Brigga and Raynor carried handheld varieties.

"The stones are still *en route*," I hissed across the courtyard.

Axel paused on the loading dock, then bent as if to tie his shoe.

"What?" he hissed back.

I held up one finger. *Torstein? Is Sverrir anywhere nearby.*

After a long pause, Torstein spoke calmly. *I don't sense any malignant presences.*

Great.

I waved Axel forward. He glanced over his shoulder before calling into the museum. "Be right back. I'm just going to check that the gate's open."

"Sounds good," said a voice from inside.

Axel jogged toward the road, then hung a sharp right before circling back toward me. "Hey."

"Hey yourself." My gaze roamed from the collared shirt that stretched across his broad shoulders to the multi-pocketed pants that hugged his thighs. "Nice outfit."

"Glad you like it." He raked one hand over his man-bun. "I can't hear you from the dock. What did you say?"

"The truck hasn't left the freeway," I said. "Torstein thinks they're still some distance away. I guess he isn't picking up on the crystals' energy, or something."

"He senses rocks? That guy is definitely out there." Axel glanced toward the trees. "Wait. How is he communicating with *you*? Did you get all that from a flash of light?"

"Uh . . ."

Axel folded his arms across his chest. I couldn't help but notice the way his biceps popped. *Mmm.*

"Ing-grid." He drew my name across two prolonged syllables. Neither one sounded happy.

"Huh?"

"How is Torstein communicating with you?" he repeated.

Just tell him. Torstein's voice made me jump. *It's only going to be worse if you wait.*

"What's wrong?" Axel whipped his head from side to side. "Is someone coming?"

Tell him, Torstein reiterated.

Be quiet!

"Why'd you jump, Shieldmaiden?" Axel's hand was on his blade. "If there's a threat, I'll—"

"It's okay." I motioned for him to stand down. "There's no one approaching. It's just . . ."

Tell. Him. Torstein was getting on my last nerve.

Fine.

"I let Torstein get in my head," I admitted.

"He's coercing you?" Fury rolled across Axel's face. "I knew he was trouble. Where is he? I'll knock some sense into—"

"No." I wrapped my hands around Axel's forearms. "I let him into my head. Literally."

"Come again?"

"We did a . . . thing," I stammered. "With the crystals. He can talk into my head. And I can talk into his."

Axel's mouth opened, closed, and opened again. "Are you telling me that maniac can read your mind?"

"Only when I let him," I said. "He said it would help us beat the dark mage."

"And you believed him?" Hurt clouded Axel's eyes. "I can't believe you wouldn't talk that over with me first."

"We're all on the same team," I reminded Axel. "We have to do everything in our power to stop our target. Even if it means going *way* outside of our comfort zones."

"If he's making you uncomfortable, so help me Odin, I'll—"

"I made this choice." My hands slid lower to squeeze Axel's tightly balled fists. "I'm okay with it. I need you to be, too."

Axel stared at me in silence. After what felt like an eternity, he said, "I don't like it. But I trust you."

"Thank you," I said quietly.

He's here. Torstein's words burned with urgency.

"What?" I blurted.

Axel tilted his head. "I didn't say anything."

113

"Torstein did." I focused inward. *What did you say?*

Sverrir is here, Torstein reiterated. *Eastern side of the nearest structure. He's moving in your direction.*

Dritt.

Language, Ingrid.

Shut it, Torstein.

I pulled my hands from Axel's and drew my sword. "He's here. The dark mage. He's on the east side of the museum, heading toward the dock."

Without a word, Axel tapped the light on his head. He pulsed three flashes toward the columns where Janna hid, and another series toward the bell tower.

It was go-time.

"Hey." Axel tucked my chin between his thumb and forefinger. He pressed lightly, angling my face upward while he brought his lips to mine. My heart thundered as he kissed me hard, his tongue sweeping across my own. I stood on tiptoe, leaning into the contact. But Axel drew back with a groan, murmuring softly as he pulled away. "Stay safe, Shieldmaiden."

"Always do." My words came on a heavy exhale. "Go. Weapon up."

Axel nodded. He took off at a sprint, charging toward the loading dock. He'd hidden his sword and bow behind a pile of boxes, and now he strapped both to his back while inching along the low brick wall to take his attack position. Movement from my right let me know Janna was in place. And a flash from the bell tower confirmed that Raynor had his arrows drawn, ready to fire.

Okay, guru, I said to Torstein. *Do your magic.*

Gladly.

Light burst across the quad. It illuminated the surrounding buildings in a brilliant white blast. A second later, pale-blue sparkles rained from the sky. The air was instantly thicker. It felt as if we'd been pushed under water, or dropped inside a thick vat of lard. I raised one arm to shield my eyes from the light, my movement noticeably slower than normal. I must have been restricted by whatever properties Torstein's spell had imbued. A second flash burst forth, and the weight suddenly lifted. The sparkles rose to form a massive orb—one that encompassed the museum, its loading dock, and all of the buildings within a half-kilometer radius. Torstein had formed his shield—one he'd promised would hold both our team and the dark mage within its boundaries. So long as our mage could sustain the dome, we'd have unimpeded access to the monster who threatened to destroy our world.

All we had to do was catch him.

Sverrir is straight ahead—at your eleven o'clock, Torstein advised.

Thanks.

I motioned with one arm, pointing slightly to my left so Janna and Axel would know where to go. Then I scooped my shield from the ground, sliding its straps around one hand and holding tight to my sword with the other. I willed my feet to move silently as I sprinted across the cobbled stones that stretched to the museum's eastern wall. The clock was ticking now.

There was no way Sverrir could have missed Torstein's magic. He had to know that he was trapped, that we'd upped our game since our last encounter, and in all likelihood, that we'd aligned with another mage. Sverrir would most definitely be on his guard. Our survival hinged upon taking him down before he set up protections we'd be unable to overcome. Time was most definitely of the essence. And we were in a fight for our lives.

Good thing I had the target in my sights.

CHAPTER 13

SVERRIR STOOD ALONE. UNARMED in the physical sense, his robe billowed in the light breeze. His back was to me, but even at a distance I noted his diminutive height, and rotund torso. He remained unmoving as I crept around the trees on silent feet. It took only seconds to reach the museum's brick wall, but in that time my heart must have pounded a thousand beats.

This time, he wouldn't get away.

When I had a clear shot, I raised my sword over my shoulder and angled it slightly downward. A quick glance to my right revealed Axel was in position. At my nod, he lifted his bow and took aim. His arrow flew through the air, its slight whistle harmonizing with the fluttering of leaves. It struck the mage between the shoulder blades with a satisfying *thwack*. Before Sverrir could turn, I was already there—sword arm up and weight transferred to my back foot. I launched forward. He stepped aside. My sword barely clipped the side of his rib cage, but the grating of metal on bone vibrated up my arm with a satisfying hum. Sverrir spun. His fingers flicked forward, as if my blow were no more than a pesky insect. An invisible punch landed squarely in my gut. My lungs emptied. I gasped for air as my torso folded. While I flew backward, Sverrir flicked again. My trajectory changed. My body was wrenched to the right. In the seconds before I struck the tree, I raised my shield and tucked my head to my chest.

The pain was instantaneous.

Explosions erupted across my left side. Tiny fissures of agony burst open, running the length of my arm to my hip. My torso pulsed, but I didn't have time for self-pity. I was falling—dropping twenty feet to the ground. The impact alone would crack whatever body part struck the pavement first. The world shifted into slow motion as I tried to swing my still-pounding hips beneath me and prayed that Tyr would grant me the grace to sustain more than ten seconds of this battle. But my body wouldn't move. It was frozen—whether locked in pain or manipulated by the dark mage's invisible blow, I couldn't tell. The only thing I knew as I soared face-first toward the ground was that severe injury was inevitable.

I hoped my team could defeat this monster without me.

My eyes widened as the pavement flew at my face. But at what should have been the moment of contact, my arms and legs shot outward. An unseen force yanked my chest upward. I hovered unsteadily, no more than half a foot separating me from the ground. A sweat droplet rolled down my nose before landing on the pavement with a soft *plop*. For a moment, the world around me was still. Quiet. Calm.

And then all Helheim broke loose.

The bright surge forced my eyes closed. A fierce wind whipped my braid against my face, and vibrations shook the ground just inches from my body. I dragged my eyes open, turning my head enough to find a veritable light show illuminating the quad. Quick flashes lit up the buildings, their lines shifting in the ever-changing light. Below me, the ground trembled. And the tree I'd just struck . . .

Oh, gods.

I can't hold you any longer. Torstein's voice thundered in my head.

So *he'd* stopped my fall.

Once you're down, you have to move. Fast!

He didn't have to tell me twice.

The pressure released from my chest. Flesh met ground with a painful thud, and I rolled to my right, the earth shaking as I moved. I leapt to my feet, readjusting my shield on my arm and trying not to panic at the wildly waving tree. Its branches swayed violently from side to side, and I nearly tripped as I scrambled out of its shadow. A bolt of lightning flashed across the sky, illuminating the dome enough that I could assess my surroundings. Behind me, Torstein was still obscured in a tree—Odin willing, a lightning-proof one. To my right, Janna raced forward, her sword drawn and her shield raised. And straight ahead . . .

Gods, no.

Ingrid! Torstein warned. *The tree!*

I turned my head just as another bolt flashed across the sky. The air parted with a deep *boom*. I watched in horror as the lightning touched just feet from where I stood. It struck the tree with a jolt, instantly filling the air with the thick scent of—

"Fire!" Brigga called from behind. "The tree's coming down! Ingrid, get out of the way!"

I lowered my head and charged into battle, racing toward the spot where Axel fought off the dark mage. A deafening crack from behind let me know the tree had fallen, but I didn't look to see how close I'd come to death-by-crushing. Sverrir stood with his back to me, lifting Axel in what appeared to be a choke hold. The dark mage was going to kill him.

There was no way I was letting that happen.

"Augh!" The battle cry left my lips as I leapt through the air. I dropped my shield arm to my side and raised my sword overhead. I brought it down on Sverrir's thigh in a swift arc, relishing the feel of blade on flesh. Axel fell to the ground as the dark mage stumbled, and I angled my weapon so it dug deeper. Sverrir raised his fingers. I brought my shield hand up. The weapon struck hard, its edge slicing into Sverrir's neck and silencing whatever incantation he'd begun to mutter. No sooner had I ripped my sword from his leg, than I was hoisted upward. The dark mage raised me with one hand and wrapped the other firmly around my neck. Panic seized my body. My mouth fell open as I struggled to breathe. My legs kicked out, but my heel had little impact on the seemingly impervious monster. Despite his short stature and jowly features, Sverrir was surprisingly strong.

And unnervingly lethal.

My vision blurred as I registered Axel's movement. The warrior dropped to the ground and swung his sword in a low arc. It clipped Sverrir's ankles. The grip on my neck loosened just enough for me to fill my lungs with air. I quickly tucked my knees to my chest and bucked forward, planting both feet firmly against the mage's chest. My kick must have startled him—he stumbled back, releasing me from his hold and falling squarely atop Axel's extended sword. The blade pierced his torso with a sickening *slurp*. I barely managed to turn my cheek before blood squirted across my face, covering my flesh in a warm, sticky film. Sverrir lay limp in Axel's arms, a sword stuck clean through his back, and a pool of blood forming neatly atop his chest. His eyes fluttered closed, and his lips flapped silently— no doubt, his effort at drawing a breath. By all accounts, it should have been a killing blow. In any normal battle, Sverrir would have been well on his way to meet Hel.

But nothing was normal when it came to destroying a mage.

Janna reached my side just as Sverrir flicked his

fingers. The two of us soared backward, landing in a heap a few feet from the burning tree. Heat pulsed at my bare arm as I rolled off my back and climbed unsteadily to my feet. Flames lapped at downed branches, the fire illuminating the dome in an eerie, orange glow. I held out my hand to lift Janna up, pulling her toward me just as a gust blew the embers our way.

"Steer clear of the fire," I shouted.

"Good call." She picked up her sword.

We squared our shoulders to the dark mage, who'd somehow managed to throw Axel into the side of the museum. The warrior struggled to right himself, while Sverrir removed the sword from his back and turned his attention to me and Janna.

We immediately dropped into attack positions.

I'll hit him with a blast from the left, Torstein pressed into my head. *If Janna strikes from the right, it will give you time to circle around. You and Axel may be able to take him down from behind, so long as . . .*

So long as what, Torstein?

So long as I can hold his attention. Torstein sounded unsure.

Great.

Where's our backup? I asked.

Brigga and Raynor have descended the bell tower and are now crossing the quad. Their presence should distract Sverrir; make it easier for me to keep his focus this way.

Okay.

I readied my sword. Odin willing, we could pull this off.

"Janna, attack from the right," I said quietly. "Torstein will keep the mage's focus while I circle around from behind."

"Affirmative. Are you sure that Torstein will—"

"*Ja*." I shuffled forward as another gust of wind blew a flaming branch across my path. "Go!"

Janna raced toward the museum's wall. She drew parallel with Sverrir, then hung a sharp right and charged. A flash of light burst from behind, drawing the dark mage's attention and giving me time to slip behind one of the trees. I crept steadily forward as Torstein threw what appeared to be white beams, and Janna launched herself at our target. In the seconds it took for me to reach Axel's side, the air grew thick with smoke while cries of pain echoed between the buildings. I forced myself not to think about *whose* cries they might have been. Instead, I wrapped my palm around Axel's forearm and pulled him upward.

"You okay?" I grunted.

"Never better." Axel rubbed his arm. A stream of blood ran from his shoulder to his elbow, its thick red stream pooling in the divots of his tricep.

"You don't look okay." I bent to pick up his sword.

"*Ja*, well." He took the offered weapon and gripped the hilt in both hands. "I've had worse."

We both raised our weapons as a series of flashes lit up the sky.

"That the good mage?" Axel asked. "Or the other one?"

"Does it matter? It's time to move."

"On your mark, Shieldmaiden."

"You're finally letting me take point?" I raised my shield to block another flash of light.

"I trained you, didn't I?" Axel shrugged. "Might as well let you show me how brilliant I am."

I rolled my eyes at Axel's ever-present ego. But I lowered my head and tucked my elbow to my side. "Sword up, Andersson."

"I like it when you take charge."

If we hadn't been in the heat of battle, I would have smacked him. As it was, I barked a determined, "Now!" before running straight at the target. Axel kept pace beside me, and I prayed that Torstein could make good on his promise to hold Sverrir's attention.

Our mage was clearly doing his best. Erratic flashes burst across the dome, interrupted by strong gusts of wind and surges of fire—whether from Torstein or nature, I wasn't quite sure. Occasionally, the flashes lasted long enough that I could see Janna. Her sword came down hard on Sverrir's head, but he waved a hand and she dropped to the ground. My captain was in trouble.

And Axel and I were still meters away.

"Faster!" I shouted over my shoulder.

Axel's blade glinted in my peripheral vision. I steeled my focus and pumped my legs harder, channeling every ounce of strength into closing the gap between us and the monster now flinging my captain into a wall. We reached him just as Janna crumbled to the ground, her low moan drowned out by a deafening clap of thunder. Clearly, Thor was on our side.

All we had to do was make him proud.

Axel jumped high in the air. He gripped his sword in two hands as he arced it overhead and drove it straight down. It pierced Sverrir's neck, sliding along the mage's spine before Axel tore it away. In the flashing light, I just made out the blood coating the blade before my own sword struck Sverrir's leg. It sliced clear to the bone, eliciting a solid *crack* as I twisted my wrist upward. The dark mage dropped to one knee. An agonized cry escaped his throat. His hand raised toward me, but Axel's sword was swift. It struck again, this time piercing Sverrir's shoulder. The mage lowered his arm. He cradled his injury and spun wildly around. Rage glinted in his eyes as he looked from Axel to me. A deadly calm settled across his face as he set the assassin in his sights and drew his fingers to his palm.

Oh, gods.

I flung myself forward, tackling Sverrir and stopping his spell before he ever saw me coming. Once he was down, I dug my fingers into his face and slammed it against the pavement. The resonant *thud* was deeply satisfying, but it would take more than one blow to stop the monster. I released the sword and jammed my thumb into Sverrir's eye. The dark mage let out a howl. A blade glinted from my left, and I shifted my gaze just as Axel delivered a crushing blow. His sword stabbed

Sverrir's bicep, pinning the arm to the ground and giving me the opening I needed. Blood coated my thumb as I pulled it from the orifice and reached out for my sword. The killing blow was within my grasp. All I had to do was take it.

The truck is nearing the dome. Torstein's voice filled my head. *Take him out, Ingrid. Now.*

With pleasure.

I lifted my sword, intent on destroying the threat to our world. But before I could strike, Sverrir's fingers twitched. His body flickered in and out of focus before disappearing beneath me. My sword hit the ground with a painful clash. Vibrations resonated along my arm as my knees collided with pavement. The dark mage was gone. We'd failed again.

What the actual Helheim?

I lifted my head and scanned my surroundings. Axel panted beside me, his sword falling to the ground as he rested his hands on his thighs. Janna paused mid-stride, shock replacing rage as she stared at the empty space beneath me. Brigga and Raynor slowed their gaits, their daggers slowly dropping from attack positions. And Torstein leapt gracefully from his tree. White sparks still flickered from his fingertips.

"Stay on guard," Torstein called out. "He's too weak to break out of the dome. He may have ported out of sight, but he has to be within the perimeter."

"You sure about that?" Axel jutted his chin.

I followed Axel's sight line to the spot where a truck approached. Its driver craned his neck out of the window, his eyes widening. I didn't blame him. The tree was still burning, the ground was cracked, and a thick film of ash coated the once-pristine courtyard. He inched his vehicle slowly forward. Just as he reached the dome's perimeter, a dark flash erupted at the edge.

Torstein swore loudly.

"What do we do?" Janna called.

"Don't let Sverrir get to those stones," Torstein shouted. "If he makes contact with even a small one, it will heal him enough to—"

SCREEECH!

The truck lurched, an unseen force pulling it within the dome. Its back doors flew open and a sea of packages spilled out. Torstein flung a beam at the chaos, but he was too late. Before the white light could reach the truck, Sverrir appeared *outside* of the barrier. He clutched a massive moonstone in one hand, a triumphant smile illuminating his battle-scarred face. The dark mage raised his other hand as he took a single step backward. With a twirl of his finger, he was gone, taking the moonstone—and all of our hopes —with him.

"No. No, no, no!" Axel roared. He turned on Torstein with a furious glare. "I thought you could contain him."

"I thought I could too." Torstein looked every bit as angry as Axel. "He was physically drained. If he hadn't made contact with the moonstone, this would have ended differently."

"Great." Axel knelt to brush a chunk of rubble from my arm. "You okay?"

"I've been better," I admitted. "But I'm not the one bleeding."

"This?" Axel eyed the blood caking along his tricep. "It's a surface wound. I barely feel it."

"Keep telling yourself that." I sought out Torstein. "Any chance you're up to healing a surface wound?"

"Of course." Torstein pointed his palm at my boyfriend. A filmy light emerged from his hand, coating Axel in a pale-pink glow. Janna watched in awe as the cut knitted itself closed, leaving behind only a thin layer of dried blood.

"Whoa," she muttered.

"I'll take care of everyone." Torstein turned his hand to Janna, then me. My body pinged as tingles rippled from my feet to my head. The pain lifted instantly before dissipating into the ether.

Axel clasped his hand around my arm and gently helped me up. He passed me my sword as I rocked unsteadily on my feet. "What the Helheim are we supposed to do now?"

"Now we recalibrate." Janna rubbed her shoulder. A burn marred its once-smooth surface. "Sverrir is one step closer to collecting what he needs, which means we're going to have to work that much harder."

Raynor lifted his face to the sky. "How?"

"I'm not sure," Janna admitted. "We had a clear shot at him and he escaped. I don't know what's left to do."

"I do." Torstein sighed. "You all need to rest. And

clear out of this area. We've made quite a mess tonight, and if you're implicated in destruction on this level, your life will get a *lot* more complicated. You'll most likely be incarcerated, which would make it very easy for Sverrir to pick you off one by one."

"Great." Janna groaned.

"We need to collect the rest of the quanta crystals before he does. Why don't you lay low for a few days while I head back to the center? I'll go over some old ground—try to narrow the search parameters at least a little based on regions I've already searched. After I've mapped out some possibilities, I'll bring you in to narrow it farther.

I shook my head. "You've been looking for years." Hundreds, if memory served. "What makes you think you'll be able to find the crystals now?"

"Because." A slow smile spread across Torstein's face. "I have something I didn't have before."

"What's that?" I asked.

Torstein's eyes locked on mine. "I have you."

CHAPTER 14

THE NEXT DAY PASSED in an exhaustion-filled blur. After the battle, we'd limped back to The Row, crawled into our beds, and slept for not nearly enough hours before the sun poked through the window. Janna, Brigga, and I had slogged our way through classes, keeping our heads low as we skirted the seemingly infinite number students gossiping about the destruction.

Overnight, the university had released a statement claiming a series of dry lightning strikes were responsible for upending the cobblestones around the museum and decimating the corners of two buildings. The same lightning was faulted for the burning of the Spartan Tree—the oldest tree on campus and a gift from the university's first president. The tree marked a major loss to the community, and students spent the better part of the afternoon laying cards and flowers at the edge of the yellow caution tape.

I felt awful. The lightning had been real, but it hadn't taken down the tree. That had had been Sverrir's doing. And if we hadn't attacked the dark mage, he wouldn't have fired those beams at a campus treasure. But even with guilt churning inside my gut, I was grateful that the school had blamed the storm for the damage we'd caused.

And I was grateful that we hadn't been caught.

Between my lack of sleep and the day's tension, I was thoroughly exhausted by the time classes ended. My feet dragged and my eyelids drooped on the walk back to the sorority. I fully intended to sleep straight through 'til morning, but Lexi had other plans.

"Good. You're back." Lexi crossed her arms as Janna, Brigga, and I trudged into the Kappa Mu foyer. She was framed by the massive vase of flowers on the entry table—the beautiful, fragrant halo surrounding her far-from-angelic head. She arched one thin brow and stared us down like a dragon who'd just pinned its prey.

Is she waiting for us?

I closed the front door behind me with a tired, "Hi, Lexi."

"The three of you might want to check your mailboxes. You'll find there's something of *great* importance inside."

"Us?" I couldn't hide my surprise. We'd never received written communications here. Most of the girls got a few letters each week, but our boxes had remained empty.

Until now.

"Uh . . . thanks." I hung a left at the round table, ignoring the smirk stretching across Lexi's face. Then I called to Janna and Brigga, "I'll grab yours too. Head upstairs and catch some rest."

"Already going," Brigga called back. "Thanks."

I quickly pulled three envelopes from our respective slots in the massive mail cubby and glanced at the fancy scrawl etched along the top. "*From The Office of The Standards Chair.* Lexi, what's this about?"

Her smirk deepened. "Open it and see."

Whatever was in this envelope, it was giving her *way* too much satisfaction. *This cannot be good.*

"Later." I headed for the stairs. "I'm too tired to deal with . . . whatever this is right now."

Lexi's eyes shot their familiar hate-daggers. "Well, be sure you're on time for Monday night dinner. Wouldn't want another black mark on your ethics record."

I didn't turn around as I climbed the stairs. I'd forgotten about the mandatory weekly dinner. Looked like my plan for a restful night had just gotten upended.

Sleep is for the weak, Ingrid.

I'd keep telling myself that.

When I dragged myself to the top of the landing, happy chaos filled its sitting area. Laughter bubbled from the pledge's room, where the girls were engaged in some kind of a sock-throwing game. Morgan and Ali chatted on the couch—each held a notebook, and they seemed to be going over a list. And Meri and Devyn, two of the officers, sat cross-legged on the floor, painting each other's fingernails. I greeted everyone as I passed, pasting a smile across my face all the while keeping my bedroom door in my sights. Thirty steps until I could plop face down on my bed, kick off my boots, and sleep until . . . well, until dinner.

Unless maybe I was *sick*? And then I could sleep straight through until—

"What are those?" Janna's voice jarred me from my daydream.

"Huh? Oh. Right." I dropped my bag and crossed to my bed, where I flopped face-first on the soft surface. Extending my arm behind me, I said, "Here. Take them. Whatever they are, they're making Lexi absurdly happy."

"That can't be good," Brigga muttered. She snatched the envelopes. Half a minute later, her gasp confirmed my assessment.

"Bad news?" Janna asked.

"We're being called in for a standards redress after Chapter tonight."

"Meaning?" I asked.

"After the chapter meetings, the officers have a second session in a closed room," Brigga said. "I've heard girls talk about it. They call those sessions 'Ethics.' They go over all the ethical violations members have committed and give them a chance to explain their actions before issuing whatever consequence they decide is best."

"But we haven't committed any ethical breaches," Janna said. "We're Valkyrians. We carry ourselves with the highest standards of honor and valor and—"

"I don't know what to tell you." Brigga set the papers on her desk. "We're being called in. Obviously, we did something to upset *someone*."

"Our existence upsets Lexi," I mumbled into my bedspread. "She's just mad Axel and Raynor aren't into her."

"Speaking of Raynor." My bed shifted as Janna sat down. "Brigga, is everything all right with the two of you?"

"What do you mean?"

I rolled my face to one side and stared at our disseminator. "She means he hasn't seemed too happy to see you flirting with Torstein. Are you into the guru now, or what?"

"He's a *light mage*." Brigga exhaled breathily. "Do you know how rare those are?"

Janna frowned. "What I know is that Raynor cares for you a great deal. He insisted on joining this mission to make sure *you* were well protected. If you don't return his feelings, that's your prerogative. But tell him sooner than later, and try not to flaunt your preference for Torstein."

"I don't think that's an issue." I yawned. "From what I can tell, Torstein's still pretty hung up on his ex. The dark mage killed her a long time ago, but I don't think he's ever really gotten over her."

"Poor thing," Brigga tutted.

"*Ja*. Well." Another yawn overtook me and I let my eyelids close. "We can talk about it later. Wake me up for dinner?"

"Of course." Janna patted my back and stood. By the time she'd reached her bed, I was already half-asleep.

I had a long night ahead of me.

Monday night dinner was the usual loud, exuberant affair. Since this was the only mandatory meal of the week, every member of Kappa Mu gathered around the big, round tables in the dining room. The event served as a communication checkpoint, with members of different houses and campus groups appearing throughout the meal to share important updates. Some messages were silly—the Beta pledges lined up to sing what Morgan later told me was a camp song, and the Zetas sent their freshman to serenade us with a horribly harmonized tune. Other groups came to invite us to participate in their holiday philanthropy projects —ornament making, gift wrapping, a food drive. The running group earned barely concealed gasps of horror when they pitched their new division, the Sunrise Run Club, and my sisters listened attentively as the student government representatives explained their timeline for spring applications.

But the most interesting announcement came right after dessert was served. I'd just tucked into a *delicious* slice of apple pie when the Alpha pledges filed into the dining room. They took their positions in two straight lines before breaking into a solemn song.

"This another camp one?" I leaned over to Morgan.

"No." Her eyes widened. "It's their chapter hymn. This is serious."

"What's a chapter hymn?" Brigga whispered.

"Their most sacred song—the one they use at initiation, and graduation, and . . . oh my god!" Morgan's hands flew to her mouth. Squeals erupted as a tall, dark-haired guy stepped around the twin lines and walked toward Kayla. He dropped to one knee in front of our president and held out his hands. He pinched something small and shiny between two fingers. As he lifted it up, gasps broke out across the room.

"What is that?" I whispered.

"His pin!" Morgan beamed. "Mike must have asked her over the weekend! This is how we formally initiate the process for a pinning ceremony!"

My eyes caught Janna's. "Kenzi said that's like, a pre-proposal?"

"Yes." Morgan sighed. "Oh, this is so romantic. It's our first pinning this year! Ooh, maybe they'll do the ceremony in December and we can make it a Christmas theme and . . ."

Morgan was off and running, planning an event I didn't quite understand and one that seemed mildly pointless. If Mike wanted to propose to Kayla, why didn't he just do *that*? They were both of eligible age— at least, they would have been in Valkyris. Why make things complicated?

"Their customs are strange." Janna spoke quietly in my ear.

"I was just thinking the same thing."

"But they do seem to make them happy. Look at her." Janna nodded at Kayla. She beamed joyfully at her boyfriend, their hands wrapped tightly together. Mike led her out of the dining room and the girls burst into boisterous applause. Excited chatter broke out, and Meri clapped her hands together to get our attention.

"You're all dismissed," she called loudly. "Chapter starts promptly at seven, so if you're not already dressed you have thirty minutes!"

The room rose as one, a sea of elated sisters bubbling about Kayla and the pinning and what they hoped *their* ceremonies might be like one day. Words like *tiara* and *ball gown* and *so many diamonds* pinged off the walls. One girl spoke of a *fairy forest*, which sounded slightly more my speed. Not that I wanted a ceremony. Or a pin. Or anything other than to capture Sverrir and go back to living a semi-normal life with my squadron. Though it *was* nice to get this much time with Axel.

We'd never been on an official mission together, and odds were good it wouldn't happen again for a long time—if ever. The Airborne Assassins and the Shieldmaiden Squadron worked tangentially, of course. We'd pool resources and evaluate threats as a unit before breaking off into our splinter groups. But it was rare for an assassin and a shieldmaiden to be part-nered like we were now. This might be our last chance to fight side by side for years—if not longer. And I liked working with Axel. He was a solid partner, and a worthy teammate . . . both on the battlefield and off. Maybe someday the two of us could even . . .

Don't go there, Ingrid. Just get through this mission. One day at a time.

Ja, but maybe . . .

All this talk of pinning had clearly driven me to madness.

"Let's go." Janna nudged my shoulder. "We'd better get changed before crazy over there finds another reason to come at us."

"Huh?" I pulled myself out of my fog. Janna and Brigga had already pushed in their chairs and were sending frosty glances at a frowning Lexi. "Oh. Right."

I shoveled one last bite of pie into my mouth before following my teammates out of the dining room. As I left, I looked over my shoulder. Lexi stood with her arms folded firmly across her chest. Irritation rolled off her furrowed brow and her narrowed eyes shot angry spears at my back. If looks could kill, I'd have been dead, wrapped, and set to sea in a blaze of flaming glory.

Thank gods she wasn't a Viking.

CHAPTER 15

"**S**ISTER BRIGGA. SISTER MORGAN.** Sister Inga." Lexi ticked names off her checklist as we filed into the chapter meeting. The long room was tucked into the sorority basement, with the officer's table set atop a small stage and rows of padded chairs for the rest of us. We'd only been to one meeting since we'd arrived. We'd pled homework fatigue on the other nights and been excused on account of needing to adjust as "exchange students." But attending Chapter was a requirement of living in the Kappa Mu house, and our goal was to blend in.

So, here we were.

"Hold up, Sister Inga."

I bristled as Lexi placed her pink-taloned hand on my shoulder. "It's Ingrid."

"Whatever. Where's your pin?"

"My what? Oh. Axel hasn't pinned me."

Nor would he, seeing as how he wasn't actually a

member of his fraternity. But Lexi didn't need to know that.

"No." Lexi narrowed her eyes. "I mean your *Kappa Mu* pin. You're not wearing it."

Becky had done the check-in at our previous meeting. She hadn't said anything about pins.

"I . . . uh . . ."

"The handbook clearly states that all sisters must wear their pins to Chapter. Otherwise, entry will be denied and an unexcused absence issued. Which, as I'm sure you're aware, results in a demerit."

"We left our pins in Norway." Janna spoke from over my shoulder. "We heard about the crime in Los Angeles, and we didn't want to travel with something so precious."

Gods, she was good.

"Yes." I quickly lowered my gaze. "We left *all* items of value behind. And since our pins are so incredibly precious to us . . ."

Lexi's lips settled in a frown. "You left behind the *one thing* you absolutely have to wear in order to attend required sorority meetings? That makes no sense."

"We do things differently back home," Janna said easily. "Surely this chapter honors cultural differences among its sisters."

"Yes, but—"

"Everything all right here?" Meri poked her head around the doorway. "Lexi, what's the holdup?"

"These three aren't wearing their pins," Lexi said

triumphantly. "That's grounds for dismissal and demerits."

"We left our pins at home—we weren't sure it would be safe to travel with them, seeing as how crime here is significantly worse than it is in Norway. And our pins are so very valuable to us." Janna spoke without a hint of insincerity.

"That's reasonable." Meri waved her hand. "Come on in. We've got a few spares upstairs—I'll see if we can get you three loaners before the next meeting."

Lexi's jaw dropped to her chest. "But—"

"You're holding up Chapter." Meri frowned. "And I have a paper due tomorrow, so move it along."

"Thanks, Meri." I pushed past Lexi and followed the sorority's social chair into the room.

"No worries. Us Nordic girls have to stick together." Meri smoothed the front of her black cocktail dress— our mandatory meeting attire. "Speaking of, I'm making my grandma's lefse this week. The really simple recipe with instant potatoes. You ladies want to join me?"

"Do we ever! I haven't had lefse in *ages*." I missed my favorite flatbread treat almost as much as I missed living in a world I knew.

Meri grinned. "My grandma just sent me a lefse pan —one of the new models from that big company in Minnesota. I can't wait to break it in."

"And I can't wait to help you," I said. "Though I should warn you, cooking's not exactly my best skill."

"Lefse's *super* easy," Meri assured me. "Well, this

recipe is at any rate. It just has to refrigerate overnight before we can roll it out. Do you use instant potatoes where you're from?"

Where I was from, potatoes hadn't even been invented yet. Or discovered. Or whatever it was one did to procure potatoes.

"We use flour," Brigga chimed in from behind. "We can swap recipes while we're cooking."

"Sounds good." Meri raised her hand in farewell before climbing the steps to the low stage at the front of the room. My friends and I slid into a row near the back. We didn't want to draw attention to the fact that we were largely unfamiliar with the sorority's customs. And if the one chapter meeting we'd attended was any indication, we were *definitely* in over our heads.

"Do you remember the prayer?" I whispered to Janna. The last meeting had opened with the group reciting some kind of chant to . . . I wasn't sure to whom.

"I think it's a spell," she whispered back.

"It's an oath." Brigga rolled her eyes. "Gods, did you two not read the handbook?"

"We read it," I said indignantly. "And I memorized key passages. Just not the prayer."

"Spell," Janna corrected.

"Oath," Brigga hissed. "Focus."

"Hey." I lowered my voice. "I got my butt handed to me last night by a seriously angry dark mage. I am bruised and bloodied and flat-out exhausted. Or, I was before Torstein healed me. But the exhausted still stands. So forgive me if I don't remember the right name for some sorority incantation."

"Oath."

"So help me Odin, Brigga, I will—"

"Sit." Janna positioned herself between us and pointed to the chairs on either side of her. "Be silent. As your senior officer, I command you both to stand the Helheim down."

I dropped into my appointed chair. "Sorry, Janna."

Sorry that Brigga's such an insufferable know-it-all.

"*Ja.* Sorry," Brigga added. She plucked a piece of paper from beneath her own chair. "And the *oath* is written out on these, in case anyone needs one."

I bent over to retrieve the parchment. Hopefully, Janna didn't see me stick my tongue out at Brigga as I moved.

Exhaustion wasn't helping me to be my best self.

"Hey, you three." Kenzi slid into the chair beside me. "Is everybody feeling zenned out after our meditation retreat yester—yikes. Looks like somebody needs a week-long stress detox."

"We didn't sleep well," Janna offered. "Too much meditation for one day."

"Usually it has the opposite effect." Kenzi laughed. "Uh-oh. We'd better be quiet—my sister looks ready to start."

I followed her gaze to the front of the room. Sure enough, Kayla stood behind the officer's table. She tapped a golden bowl with a small, wooden stick—no doubt a gift from her yoga-loving sister. A melodious chime sounded throughout the room, and the cheerful chatter dissipated into silence.

"Welcome, ladies." Kayla looked out over the chairs. "Looks like we've got a full house tonight."

"Congratulations, Kayla!" someone hollered from the middle of the room. "You're getting *pinned*!"

Kayla's smile stretched from ear to ear. "We'll discuss social matters when we get to that item on the agenda." She beamed. "But thanks. I'm excited!"

"How did he ask you?" another girl spoke up from the left.

"On a hike." Kayla blushed. "We'd had brunch with his parents, and he took me out to the forest where he had this gorgeous picnic set out and he just . . . asked me!"

"She was so excited last night," Kenzi whispered. "I've never seen her look so happy."

"That's great." I smiled at my friend.

"But let's take care of business before we get to our *fun* agenda items." Kayla sat and picked up her pen. "Cara, do we have any house issues?"

"Housekeeping item number one: chores." Cara glanced at her parchment. "I've just posted this week's list by the mailboxes, so check out where your pledge class has been assigned. Chores must be completed no later than eight p.m., except for mail which should be placed in our individual cubbies no later than five. Any questions?"

Nobody raised their hands.

"Good. Housekeeping item two." Cara wrinkled her

nose. "The raccoon problem is definitely getting worse." Cara scribbled on her parchment. "I'll talk to campus maintenance—let them know the population seems to be expanding. In the meantime, seal up our garbage cans *every time you use them*. Understood?"

A sea of cocktail-dress-clad girls nodded their agreement.

"Great. That's all for me, Kayla. We can go to item two."

Kayla consulted the agenda in front of her. "Next up is our philanthropy chair. Blair?"

A girl I hadn't yet met stood up at the head table. Her beaded, black dress and long, braided hair gave her an earthy vibe—not unlike that of our seers back home. I was surprised I hadn't seen her at Kenzi's dawn meditation class.

"Thanks, Kayla." Blair picked up her parchment. "Most of you have already gotten in the majority of your volunteer hours—so, well done, you guys. If you're short, please consider taking a leadership role in our Dodge Climate Change fundraiser next month. We still need someone to organize the dodgeball tournament brackets, and a stager/decorator who can transform the front lawn into a winter wonderland."

"What's dodgeball?" I whispered to Kenzi.

"Do you not have that in Norway?" Kenzi shook her head. "Lucky."

"What is it?"

"We hurl bouncy balls at people and try to knock them out of the game. The last person to avoid being

145

hit wins." Kenzi shuddered. "It's going to be our fall fundraiser. We're renting machines and covering the playing field in snow. Should be interesting to see all the guys try to take each other out without falling over."

"Fraternities do the tournament too?" I asked.

"It's open to everyone. That's how we raise money," Kenzi said. "Any team of five who comes up with the registration fee can enter."

"Ah."

"Anyway, come see me if you want to sign up for the planning committee." Blair spoke from the front. "Oh, and if you can't pitch in there and you're still behind on hours, don't worry—remember, you can participate in another house's philanthropy for up to half of your Kappa Mu hours. Just be sure to let me know what you did, and I'll mark you off after I confirm with their house's chair."

"Thank you, Blair." Kayla scanned her agenda. "Winter Formal's up next, so I'll turn things over to our social chair."

Meri stood. "We're just a few weeks away from the biggest social event of the semester—the Winter Formal. The committee and I have been working tirelessly to secure a great deal on an amazing location, and I am pleased to tell you that this year we'll be dancing the night away at none other than the world renowned Hotel del Coronado."

A cheer swept across the room.

"I love that place," a high-pitched voice squealed.

"Oh my god, did you see what they did with it last Christmas?" another chimed in.

"Didn't Marilyn Monroe live there?" someone gasped. "Wait, that was the Roosevelt."

Meri held up her hands. "We're ironing out the final details, but look for updates in your mailboxes over the next week or two. Dress is black-tie optional, of course, and we'll secure a block of rooms so we don't have to drive all the way back here that night. Everyone will be paired with their roommates, but if you want to secure your own accommodations, you're welcome to do so. Just let me know so I can release your room."

"I can't wait." Kayla clapped her hands together.

"Me neither," Meri admitted. "Oh, and I'll be meeting with the Alpha's social chair this week to organize a certain pinning ceremony, so if anyone has any ideas, come to me after the meeting and I'll take down your notes."

Kayla's cheeks pinked. "Thanks, Meri. Okay, last up is our spring rush. I know it feels like we *just* got through our last recruitment, but it's time to gear up again. Rush chair, where are we in the process?"

Devyn stood beside Kayla. "Spring rush kicks off the third week in January—just one week after we get back from winter break. It seems like a way off, but it's going to be here before we know it. The rush committee is in the process of firming up our theme days, our recruitment events, and the total number of pledge spots we can offer based on Ali's financial report. Given we only have a few graduating seniors this year, we don't have a ton of live-in spots for the next school year. So, we're really only looking to take on five, maybe eight pledges this spring. Fall will be bigger, as always, but this time around we're going to have to be highly selective in our offers."

"We are always highly selective," Kayla pointed out.

"True," Devyn agreed. "But it'll be an *extra*-small class next semester. Good news is that we'll only need to fill a few big sister spots, so if you're looking to take on a little let me know and I'll put you on the list."

"What's a little?" I whispered to Kenzi.

"All new pledges are assigned a big sister to help guide them through their first year in the house. The pledges are the littles—little sisters." Kenzi arched her brow. "Don't you do bigs and littles in Norway?"

"We do," I said quickly. "Sorry, language barrier."

"No worries." Kenzi smiled.

Whew.

"Does anybody have any additional business for our chapter? Anything you want us to address? No?" Kayla looked around the room. "If that's the case, I think we can dismiss for the night. If you got an Ethics note, give us a few minutes to finish things here and then wait in the library. We've got a short list this week, so we should be done pretty quickly. Thank you *all* for behaving yourselves. You make us proud—and more importantly, you make Lexi's job boring!"

The ethics chair rolled her heavily lined eyes. "My job is *never* boring."

"Either way, you're *so* well suited to it," Kayla said

sweetly. "Now, please rise and join me in singing our closing convocation—the Kappa Mu Song of Sisterhood."

She pressed a button on her phone. A cavalcade of horns filled the air, and the room broke into harmonious song. I mouthed words as I picked them up, trying not to giggle as Janna flapped her mouth open and closed like a fish. Luckily, nobody turned around.

And thankfully, Lexi was too far away to read our non-synchronized lips. Odin only knew what she'd do if she ever figured out we *truly* did not belong here.

CHAPTER 16

"**W**HAT ARE YOU IN** for?" A tall brunette stuck out her hand. I'd seen her around the house, but we'd never actually met. "I'm Tara, by the way."

"Ingrid." We shook. I pointed to my friends, who'd taken seats beside me in the library. "This is Janna and Brigga. And we're not sure."

"You don't know why you've been called to standards?" Tara waggled her fingers. "Let me see your slip."

Janna passed over the piece of paper with *From The Office of The Standards Chair* printed across the top.

Tara scanned it quickly, then returned it with a shrug. "That's weird. Lexi and Becky are supposed to tell you why you're here. Sometimes it's a mistake, and that way you have a few hours before your hearing to gather your defense."

"Gather our defense?" Janna shot me a look. "Are we on trial?"

"Kind of." Tara dropped into a seat across the table. "You're the Norway girls, right? Don't you have standards there?"

How to answer, how to answer . . .

"We are expected to hold ourselves to stringent codes of behavior," I said honestly. "But we don't have a peer review group, per say."

If we had, then during our Academy days, Brigga would have been called in every day of the week and twice on Thor's Day. She'd definitely cleaned up her act since graduation.

"Interesting." Tara stared at the ceiling. "I guess Norwegian K. Mu's are just better behaved than L.A. ones."

"Maybe." Janna folded her hands together. "So, this trial. Will we be ejected from the house if we fail to mount an adequate defense?"

"Oh, nothing like that." Tara laughed. "You'll probably just get a demerit and have to do whatever menial task Lexi deems appropriate. Like wash her car, or clean the bathroom in Pledge Porch, or something."

"Ew." Brigga wrinkled her nose.

"You've never cleaned a bathroom?" I asked.

"I have not," she said proudly.

"The disseminators have staff," Janna whispered in my ear.

"Of course they do." I sighed. Unlike Valkyris' information sorters, shieldmaidens were expected to clean our own quarters—including our private bathing rooms. I could only imagine what Pledge Porch's communal facility would be like, seeing as it was shared by sixteen girls . . .

Lexi better not have an actual case against us.

I turned to Janna. "How do we defend ourselves against a charge we don't even know?"

"Lexi will have to tell you why you're here once your meeting begins," Tara offered. "She and Becky always read the complaint—"

"Complaint?" Brigga asked.

"We're all here on account of someone in the house complaining about something they think we've done," Tara explained. "Sara here drank one too many at the exchange last week and puked all over our housemother's azaleas."

"I said I was sorry!" A pink cheeked girl ducked her head as she entered the library. "And Gertrude said she forgave me!"

"Tell that to Lexi." Tara shrugged. "She's got to hit her quota of charges for the month. Otherwise, Becky will go for her job."

"Wait. So, that's why we're here?" Janna frowned. "Because Lexi has to bring in a certain number of people?"

"That makes sense," I said. "Lexi hates us. If she has to hit numbers, she may as well torture the people she doesn't like."

"That's an ethical breach in and of itself," Tara said. "She could lose her chair if the officers felt she was using her position for anything other than the greatest good of the sorority. She must have a valid reason for calling you in. Have you pulled a Sara?"

"Hey!" Sara piped up.

"Sorry. Have you, uh, engaged in *conduct unbecoming a member of Kappa Mu?*" Tara corrected.

"Not better," Sara muttered.

"Tell that to Gertrude's azaleas," Tara teased.

Sara buried her face in her hands.

"We've been on time to dinners and classes, and hit our study hours and kept our room clean." I shrugged. "I can't think of any infractions that we've committed."

That Lexi knows about.

"No curfew violations? Nothing?" Tara asked.

"Well . . ." I bit on my bottom lip. We'd been a *little* bit late coming home last night. Saving the world from the wrath of a dark mage had taken slightly longer than expected. But nobody had seen us slip in. And we'd closed our door before we left, so for all anyone knew, we'd just gone to bed early.

Right?

"Ah. That's it, then." Tara nodded. "They've really been cracking down on curfews this year. It's an easy demerit for them to issue, so it ups Lexi's count and makes her look good to national."

"Right." I glanced at Janna. "Um, so, is there a solid defense to a curfew violation? Theoretically?"

"Family emergency?" Tara offered.

How about stopping a time-traveling magic-wielder from procuring the tools he needs to wipe us from existence?

"We don't really have local family," Janna pointed out.

"I'll handle her." Brigga narrowed her eyes. "I know a thing or two about mean girls."

"I'll say," I muttered.

"Gee, thanks," Brigga said.

"Because of how you *used* to be. Trust me, you have mellowed *considerably* since we graduated."

"Again, thanks." Brigga rolled her head from side to side. "But *ja*. I get girls like Lexi. I can definitely take her on."

"Tara?" Meri appeared in the doorway. "The committee will see you first."

Tara stood and walked out of the library. When she got to the doorway, she turned around and whispered over her shoulder. "You'd better hope so, Brigga. Lexi's been on a real mean streak for the past few weeks. Nobody's come out of standards with an absolution since, well, since before you three got here."

"You don't say." A slow smile crept across Brigga's face. For a moment, she almost looked like the old Brigga—the one who'd delighted in torturing my friends and I during our time at Valkyris Academy. Her vicious rumors, snarky comments, and scholastic sabotage had made our lives sheer and utter misery on multiple occasions.

I couldn't wait to see her take on Lexi.

CHAPTER 17

"**T**HE COMMITTEE WILL SEE you now." Meri waved at me from the doorway.

I pushed myself to my feet and followed Janna and Brigga out of the library.

"I have to admit, I was surprised to see your names on the agenda. But I haven't had a chance to read the agenda. What are you in for?"

"We're not sure." Janna held out her ethics slip. "Lexi didn't tell us."

Meri frowned. "Come in and let's talk. I'm sure we can straighten this out." She opened the door and motioned for us to step inside.

We filed into the sitting room where Kayla, Ali, and Becky were nestled into a single couch. Lexi held the place of honor in a leather armchair to their right, while Meri crossed to the chair opposite the mistress of misery.

"Let's get started." Meri pointed to the couch that

formed the fourth side of the seating square. Janna, Brigga, and I took our places. "Lexi, will you please read the charge so our sisters know why they've been called tonight?"

"Hold on." Kayla raised one pink-and-white-tipped finger and turned to face Lexi. "You haven't told them their charge? That's not procedure."

Lexi raised her chin. "This particular charge is fairly unique. I didn't want to give them a chance to concoct some half-baked alibi and further sully Kappa Mu's good name."

Missing curfew is that *big of a deal these days?*

"Lexi." Kayla frowned. "We have *never* brought a girl in without first disclosing our reason. That's just mean. Not to mention a violation of the protocol you swore to uphold as ethics chair."

"You might want to press pause on that judgment until you've heard the charge."

"I noticed it's not on our agenda." Kayla's frown deepened. "But I thought that was just an oversight. If it was deliberate, and you've further breached protocol by deceiving the officers, then—"

"Kayla. Trust me." Lexi crossed her long legs. Her black mini-skirt slid higher up her thigh. "You're going to find this *very* interesting."

"I'd better." Kayla raised a steaming mug from the table beside the couch and took a sip. "Go on."

"Last night, the sisters in question arrived home at twelve-thirty a.m.—fifteen minutes past the designated curfew."

"This is about another curfew violation?" Kayla stared at Lexi. "Seriously?"

"Yes." Lexi smirked. "These three have brought a lot of attention to our house. You saw what happened to our social calendar when we announced we'd be hosting sisters from Norway. Every frat wants an exchange with us, every sorority suddenly wanted to attend our dodgeball fundraiser. With that kind of attention on Kappa Mu, it's imperative that we hold ourselves to the highest possible standard. What one member does reflects on the whole of the house. It says so in our bylaws."

"True," Kayla conceded. "But seeing as this is their first curfew infraction, it's possible they actually had a reason."

"We did," Brigga spoke up. "We were at the library."

Technically, we *had* been at the library yesterday— we'd commandeered a study room for our battle-strategy session. Brigga had just fudged the timeline.

"You were at the library at midnight on a Sunday?" Lexi questioned.

"Yes. We were studying and we fell asleep." Brigga didn't blink.

"We're really sorry," Janna offered. "We promise it won't happen again."

"It shouldn't have happened the first time," Lexi said. "Our chapter has a *very* strong reputation as being among the most upstanding on The Row. The three of you seem to have very little regard for our rules. Just because you're not from here doesn't mean you deserve any special treatment. You have a duty as a Kappa Mu to uphold the same standards as the rest of us. Which is why I—"

"Excuse me." Brigga stared Lexi down. "But being fifteen minutes late for one curfew hardly counts as disregarding rules. I think there's something else going on here."

Lexi's eyes flashed. "And what would that be?"

"You don't like us." Brigga leaned forward. "You've had a problem with us from day one. You were rude to us when we first arrived at Kappa Mu, you were rude to us the night of the Halloween party, and you've been rude to us every day since. You've threatened us with demerits for things other sisters do without thought, and you've made it more than clear that you don't want us here—maybe because of the fact that we *do* draw attention to this house. Attention you'd rather be directed at you."

"That is completely false," Lexi gritted.

"Which part?"

"All of it. I have been nothing but welcoming. And that you'd suggest otherwise—"

"Please," Brigga scoffed. "You obviously have a problem with us. And it seems to me that you're using your position as ethics chair to execute some kind of personal vendetta against us. Which, I'm pretty sure, violates the very standards that you're supposed to protect. No?"

"Lexi? Is that true?" Meri frowned. "Are you abusing your position?"

"No." Lexi glared at Brigga. "The fact is that these three seem to think that they're above our rules. They missed curfew. They should be disciplined just like every other member."

"We admitted to missing curfew," Janna said. "And we apologized."

"We were fifteen minutes late. Big deal. Everyone's allowed to make a mistake." Brigga crossed her arms. "You know, this is why Axel and Raynor couldn't wait to get away from you at that Halloween party. You remember, Lexi—the night you threw yourself at them?"

"I did no such—"

"You did," Brigga said matter-of-factly. "You pretty much offered yourself up right there. Where we're from, that kind of behavior is considered tacky. And just a little feedback—Axel and Raynor were *not* impressed."

"This is highly inappropriate considering that *you* are the one who's—"

"Let me give you a little tip," Brigga said. "Women in Norway know that when a man goes to his hunting cabin and a moose shows up on his porch, he'll shoot the moose. Why wouldn't he? It's there, and it's an easy kill, right? But once he's done, he'll step right over that carcass and go into the forest to find a moose he actually has to work for. Men are in this for the *hunt*. Not just the kill."

Lexi's eyes narrowed. "Are you comparing me to a moose?"

"I'm saying that guys don't respect girls who are easy. At least, Axel and Raynor don't. I mean, the way you practically throw yourself at them . . ." Brigga shook her head. "Desperation's not a good look on you."

Lexi's nostrils flared. "And lying's not a good look on you."

"Oh, I'm not lying." Brigga smirked. "Raynor gave me an earful after that party. He told me he'd never seen anyone who clearly valued themselves so little and who—"

"You're *lying*," Lexi seethed, "about being in the library. You weren't late because you fell asleep. You were late because you were vandalizing school property!"

Oh, gods.

Ali sucked in a breath. "That's a serious accusation, Lexi."

"We have a witness." Lexi turned triumphantly to her second. "Tell them, Becky."

Wait. Was Becky there?

The deputy ethics chair shifted in her seat. "Well, you know those lightning strikes last night? The ones that allegedly did all the damage to the buildings and the ground on campus?"

"That storm was *freaky*," Kayla said. "I've never seen lightning in L.A.! Well, once during Freshman year. But it's so rare—we *never* get weather like that. I didn't even know dry lightning was a thing!"

"Me neither," Ali added.

"Dry lightning may be a thing, but do you really think it's what burned down the oldest tree on campus?" Lexi asked. "When lightning strikes, it's supposed to hit the tallest thing around, right? Why would it hit that tree when there are way bigger buildings nearby?"

"Stop right there." Kayla raised one finger. "Are you accusing our sisters of arson?"

Lexi cleared her throat. "Just tell everyone what you saw."

"Okay." Becky played with her cuticles. "So, when I was walking home from the library last night—where I *actually* was because I had a paper due today—I saw the flashes over by the museum."

No. No, no, no . . .

"It was too late for an event, so I knew they weren't strobe lights. But they do film a lot of stuff on campus, so I went to see what show it was. I figured maybe I could meet a cute actor or something. Like those brothers in that new series with—"

"Stay on point," Lexi snapped.

"Sorry. Right. Anyway, I got there and there weren't any cameras—that I could see, anyway. Maybe it was one of those hidden camera shows or something, because honestly, the whole thing seemed too out there to be real—"

"Becky!"

"Right." Becky blushed. "Anyway, the lights were *really* bright. There was this one big flash, and it lit up the whole area, and that's when I saw Brigga. She and

Raynor were running out of the bell tower. They must have been making out or something because their faces were all flushed. But what was weird was they were both carrying some kind of knife—like, daggers or something."

Oh, gods. Oh, gods. Oh, gods.

"And what about the others?" Lexi pressed. "Ingrid and Janna?"

"Like I said, the lights were *really* bright. It was super hard to make out what was going on. But yeah, I saw Janna too. I think. She was behind a tree, holding a sword."

How the Helheim are we going to get out of this one?

"You mean to tell us," Meri said slowly, "that you think Janna—*our Janna*—was carrying a sword during a lightning storm in the middle of the night?"

"Janna is the sweetest, calmest girl." Kayla frowned. "She does *yoga* with my sister, for heaven's sake. Why would a pacifist carry a weapon?"

Hope bubbled in my heart.

"Yes, Becky. Why?" Meri turned to Lexi's second-in-command.

"I don't know." Becky shrugged. "Like I said, it was late, and the storm was going, and maybe I just imagined the whole thing."

"You did not!" Lexi objected. "You saw what you saw. These three carrying weapons, wreaking destruction on campus, and out past curfew while *not at the library*."

"Technically, she only thinks she saw two of them,"

Ali pointed out. "Becky, was Ingrid a part of this . . . scene?"

I held my breath. If I understood the timing, I'd been in the middle of stabbing the dark mage when Becky had come by. If she'd witnessed me in the act of attempted mur—

"I didn't see Ingrid," Becky admitted.

Air whooshed from my chest. *Thank gods.*

"But the three of them are always together," Becky continued. "I figure she was somewhere close by."

"Thank you, Becky." Lexi raised her chin triumphantly.

"Yes. Thank you." Meri tapped her fingers against the arm of her chair. She and Kayla exchanged a *look*. After a moment, the president nodded, and Meri turned her attention to Becky. "Thank you for confirming what this committee has suspected for some time."

The blood stilled in my veins. Were they on to us? Were we about to be outed because Becky just happened to be in the right place at the wrong time? I inched my fingers toward Janna's and held tight to her hand. Our weapons were upstairs. We'd have to run for our closet if we wanted to retrieve them before—

"Becky, I'm sorry. But your drinking has gotten out of control." Meri stared the deputy down.

Wait. What?

"We let it slide because we knew you were doing your best to follow the house guidelines, but this is just too much. Swords? Daggers? Arson? What kind of sorority subterfuge do you think these three are engaged in?"

Becky's mouth fell open. "I—"

"These girls are our *guests*, Becky. Our guests." Kayla frowned. "And we do not accuse guests of committing felonies."

"I never said anything about—"

"It's just too much," Meri said. "We appreciate everything you've done for this committee, but I think it will be best for everyone if you take a step back. At least for the time being."

Kayla placed her hand on Becky's arm. "We want you to get the help you need. My mom knows all the best energetic healers in L.A.—if you want to do a detox or go to a more intense treatment facility, I'm sure one of her contacts can get you a referral."

"I wasn't drinking last night!" Becky objected. "I know it sounds crazy, but I really did see Brigga running with a weapon. Janna too . . . I'm pretty sure."

"Becky told me this same story the second she got home," Lexi vowed. "And she was completely sober. I swear to you."

"About that." Meri and Kayla exchanged another look. "Kayla, you'd better take this one. It's a bit more . . . delicate."

"Of course." Kayla looked sadly at Lexi. "Listen, you've been under a lot of stress lately. K. Mu National upped the number of charges you're expected to issue, and you've had to crack down on things we used to let slide. It's hard to be the sorority bad cop. Trust me, I understand."

"I am more than meeting my duties, if you're suggesting that I—"

"I'm not saying anything about your duties," Kayla said. "You're a firm enforcer, and you've held this house to the high standards both national *and this board* expect of our members. For that, we are incredibly grateful."

Lexi narrowed her eyes. "But?"

"But this accusation . . . it's extreme. Even for you."

"I know. But when one of our sisters witnesses behavior unbecoming a Kappa Mu—"

"I think we've established that witness is unreliable," Meri said gently.

"I wasn't drinking!" Becky objected. "I had a paper due in the morning! I was working in the library—I swear!"

"Brigga." Kayla turned to my teammate. "Were you making out with someone in the bell tower last night, like Becky suggested?"

"I was *not* making out in the bell tower," Brigga swore.

Which was technically the truth.

"And Janna. Did you set fire to the Spartan Tree?"

"I did no such thing," Janna vowed.

Again, true. That one was on Sverrir.

"I thought not." Kayla set her mug on the table. "Lexi, you had to know the arson/weapons charge wasn't going to stick. I'm curious, what was your proposed consequence for the fact that they may have missed curfew?"

"They *did* miss curfew." Lexi's eyes narrowed to slits.

"They admitted as much," Ali pointed out. "That's not in question. I think Kayla's just trying to figure out the severity of the punishment you wanted on that charge alone."

"Obviously, the same as any other sister. A demerit." Lexi practically drooled over the word. "With the understanding that as *guests* in our home, they'll be held to the American custom of three strikes. Two more infractions, and they'll be booted from the house."

"Whoa." Ali held up her hands.

"That's not how the demerit system has *ever* worked here," Meri said.

Kayla shook her head. "It's pretty clear to this committee that you've got some kind of a personal issue with our exchange sisters. It has not escaped our notice that you've been . . . less than welcoming to them."

"I'm not falling at their feet like the rest of you, if that's what you mean."

"It seems to go deeper than that." Kayla fingered the tips of her jet-black hair. "You don't like them. I get it. Sounds like you made a play for their guys, and you got blown off. Nobody likes to be rejected—especially by guys as hot as those two Vikings. Not that I'm trying to objectify anyone," she added.

"Axel and Raynor wouldn't be offended," I said. "Trust me."

"Good. Because we take harassment *very seriously* here." Kayla turned her attention back to Lexi. "All kinds of harassment."

Lexi glowered. "If you're thinking that I have somehow intimidated these ... these ..."

"I'm thinking that you've let your personal feelings interfere with your job as ethics chair. That's something each one of us swore wouldn't happen when we took the vow to serve Kappa Mu. I've heard from *very* trustworthy sources that you've singled Janna, Ingrid, and Brigga out for unfavorable treatment."

"I have not," Lexi objected.

"Oh?" Kayla blinked. "So you *didn't* threaten them with demerits for not attending a non-mandatory exchange?"

"I—well, I mean, I ... they were ... ugh!"

"Exactly." Kayla crossed her legs at the ankles. "I'm sorry, Lexi. But you really need to evaluate whether this position is the best use of your talents. If you can't be impartial, then we're going to have to ask you to step down."

"Excuse me?" Lexi balked.

"Why don't you take the weekend to think about it," Meri said calmly. "Abuse of power is a *serious* violation of our oath, and it's one we hope you're not looking to repeat."

Venom spewed from Lexi's eyes. Most of it was directed at me.

Gulp.

"As for the three of you . . ." Kayla turned to Janna. "You admitted to breaking curfew, so we do have to issue a demerit. But *like everyone else*, you can have that demerit removed from your record by performing an act of sisterly service. What do you think about serving at the alumni tea this weekend? Sound like a reasonable reparation?"

Janna nodded. "We accept your consequence and look forward to making amends."

"Excellent. In that case, you're free to go." Kayla stood and crossed to the door. "I'll bring the next case in. Lexi, Becky, you guys need to take a minute?"

"No," Lexi spat.

Becky just shook her head, clearly miserable.

I pushed myself to my feet. "Right. Well, then. Thank you for, uh . . . this."

Janna and Brigga stood and walked to the door. I followed quickly, eager to clear out of the tension-filled room. As I stepped through the doorway, I looked over my shoulder. Lexi sat ramrod straight in her chair, her heavily lined eyes shooting hate-daggers my way. The corners of my mouth tugged up in an icy smile as I rounded the corner and marched down the hall.

Lexi may have come to play. But so had we.

And you didn't mess with a shieldmaiden.

CHAPTER 18

O N WEDNESDAY AFTERNOON, TORSTEIN
sent a car to bring Janna, Brigga, Axel, Raynor,
and I out to Malibu. Traffic was only mildly awful,
which meant that the sun still shone brightly as we
walked across the lawn that bordered the parking lot.
Its rays reflected off the pristine blue ocean, projecting
a calm I knew wasn't reflected in the wild waters
beneath.

"This is Torstein's place?" Raynor's head whipped
from the ocean to the enormous glass palace. "How
much money is in mage-ing?"

"It's his meditation center," I reminded him. "He
runs his business out of here. It isn't his house."

Though come to think of it, I didn't know where he
lived. Maybe there were residences over on the cottage
side?

"Whatever it is, it is *nice*." Axel slung his arm around

my shoulders. "So, where is the guy? He said he had an update for us."

"And I do." Torstein emerged from the center. He wore the standard uniform of all white—loose pants and a sleeveless, fitted shirt. He was leaner than Axel and Raynor, but the muscles of his arms still popped as he held out his hands. "Welcome, fellow souls, to the Spiritual Center for Meditation. I'm pleased the clouds held off for your arrival. How lovely is this view?"

"It's beautiful," Brigga chirped. "*Hei*, Torstein."

The guru folded his hands and bowed.

"I do hope you're hungry," Torstein said. "I've asked the staff to set a table for us on the north lawn. We have much to discuss, and it's always best to strategize over a good meal. Don't you agree?"

Beside me, Axel's torso straightened. "I do."

"Wonderful. Follow me." Torstein turned on bare feet and walked around the front of the center. The sun reflected off the glass windows, and I turned my head as we rounded the corner and headed toward the northern end of the compound.

"I miss living on the ocean." Axel stared at the sea. "I can't wait until this mission's completed and we can go home. See trees. Swim in *that*."

I tilted my head to look at him. "I don't remember you being a particularly enthusiastic swimmer. Odin knows you're not the best rower."

"That was one time, Ingrid. One time you had to row because I—"

"I know. I know." I raised my hands in surrender.

"You were injured. Otherwise you'd have been *so* much more helpful on that long journey home from Clan Bjorn."

"Yes." Axel slid his arm over my back and pulled me into him. "I would have. And don't forget—*I* saved *you*."

I laughed. "Keep telling yourself that."

Heat crept up my neck as Axel lowered his head to mine. Our lips met in a slow, lingering, knee-buckling kiss.

Gods, Axel was good at this.

"You two planning on joining us?" Raynor shouted.

I reluctantly pulled back.

"We're on duty." I sighed. "Better keep moving."

"Fine." Axel kissed me again, then slipped his arm around my shoulders and led me along the grass. "But the minute we're off, Shieldmaiden . . ."

"Big plans for me, huh?" I teased.

Axel's emerald eyes deepened a shade. "You have no idea."

Mmm . . .

We followed the others along the lawn, turning right at the dirt walkway that led toward the cottages and ending up in a spot I hadn't seen before. Green grass butted against a towering rock formation. It offered a respite from the light breeze that swept off the ocean, so the air was slightly warmer than it had been along the cliffs. Potted palms formed a circle around a long table that had been set with linens, plates, silverware, and too many food platters to count. Mountains of bread were piled alongside clusters of cheese, fruit, and vegetables. One enormous platter contained heaps of cured meats, while another had what appeared to be an entire side of beef cut into thin slices. There were baskets of lefse, and towers of waffles, and even a dish of gently steaming salmon. My stomach rumbled as Axel and I took our places behind two chairs.

"Thank you all for joining me today." Torstein waved his hand toward the feast. "Please sit. Eat. Martin and Marius, you may go. I'll call for you should we need anything else."

Two white-clad men slipped discretely from their positions against the rocks. They walked silently toward the cottages, ducking into one I assumed was their quarters. Or maybe it was the kitchen. I still knew so little about this place.

Or Torstein.

"Let me give us a bit of privacy." Torstein flicked his fingers. A faint mist settled around the table in an arc, shimmering slightly before blinking out of existence.

"What was that?" Axel asked.

"We're shielded. Our voices are now inaudible beyond the barrier. If we're going to talk business, I prefer that it be in private." Torstein pulled out his chair and sat. He motioned for the rest of us to do the same.

"Good." Janna took her seat. "So, what's your status? The last time we met, you were planning to investigate potential crystal locations."

"And I have." Torstein frowned. "I've scanned much

of Southern California over the years, and nothing ever turns up. But yesterday I noticed something different. A low pulse emanated from the Palos Verdes area. It was out of alignment with the crystals in my possession, but the frequency was similar enough in pitch that I went to investigate."

"You, uh . . . *hear* crystals?" Axel and Raynor exchanged a look.

"Yes." Torstein handed Axel a platter of meat. "Please. Eat."

Axel forked several slices onto my plate before serving himself.

"Thanks." I spooned herb-covered potatoes on both of our plates and passed them to Janna. "So, what did you find in . . . Pillows Verdes?"

"*Palos* Verdes." Torstein smiled. "And nothing. There wasn't anything out of the ordinary whatsoever. I don't know if I misread the energy, or if something *was* there and it left. But there wasn't so much as a trace by the time I made it down the coast. I suppose that's what I get for taking the freeway."

Traffic in the future was no joke.

"What are the next steps?" Janna passed the salmon to Brigga.

"We wait until I get another hit and then investigate together. I'm convinced that pulse was something—the pitch is too unique."

Axel cut into his meat. "I don't like waiting around."

"Neither do I," I agreed. "Odin only knows what Sverrir is doing."

"It can't be much," Torstein pointed out. "He doesn't have all of the ingredients, which means he has to stay here. Until he collects them, we at least know where he is."

"And when he is." I shook my head. "He jumps through time. Gods, the chaos he could create if . . ."

"Don't go there." Raynor lowered his fork. "If we had some sense of his motivation, maybe we could anticipate his next moves. I wish we knew *why* he was doing all of this. Why does he want to control the realms?"

"And what could possibly make him want to erase *very important* parts of the past?" I bit furiously into my salmon.

"You don't know?" Torstein looked up in surprise. "You've traveled all this distance to fight him without knowing why?"

I caught Janna's eye and arched my brow. When she nodded, I dabbed my napkin to my mouth and turned toward Torstein. "I told you that we're from Norway," I said carefully. "And I'm guessing you picked up that we're a bit out of our era here, just like you."

Torstein picked up his glass. "I've deduced as much."

"Well, while you've lived through multiple centuries, we, uh, haven't." I bit my bottom lip. "We're only as old as we look. We traveled through time to get here."

"How?" Torstein stared at me curiously. "I know Sverrir has utilized herbs to make jumps, but you're not mages. Are you?"

"We aren't," I confirmed. "We're warriors—well, the four of us are. Brigga is a disseminator—a collector of information. We live on a beautiful island in Norway, where men and women are equals, resources are shared, and the greatest good of the greatest number is prized above individual gain. We're from Valkyris."

Torstein's glass froze halfway to his mouth. "Valkyris?"

"Yes." I nodded. "It's a utopian society in what's apparently called the Viking Era—"

"I know about Valkyris," Torstein said.

He did?

"How?" Raynor asked. "We only just went public in our time. Are we more outspoken in the future or—"

"Valkyris is the reason Sverrir is here." Torstein set his glass on the table. "Yours is the society he's working to destroy."

"We know," Axel said drily. "We found his to-do list back at his old camp. Destroying our home was item number one."

"How do *you* know that?" Janna set her utensils down.

"Because I was there for the war of the mages." Torstein leaned forward. "And I heard him make the vow to destroy your world."

CHAPTER 19

"**Y**OU DID WHAT NOW?**" I blinked at the entirely-too-calm guru. "You were there when he . . . there was a vow . . . you . . ."

"Back the fishing boat up." Axel released his utensils. "What exactly do you know?"

"Let's start at the beginning." Torstein placed his napkin on the table. "The war of the mages went on for weeks—far longer than any of us had anticipated. What started in subterfuge quickly progressed to open warfare. We all knew the astronomical alignment was coming, and neither side could agree on the best way to harness the powers. Our side, of course, wanted a stone that would cloak the earth in celestial energy— raise the collective consciousness to ensure positive planetary evolution. Our opponents wanted a crystal to open dark portals."

"Dark portals?" Brigga whispered.

"Do those really exist?" Raynor asked.

"They do," Torstein said. "And they were at the heart of the mage war."

"Go on," I urged.

"On the morning of the alignment, I took a walk along the sea caves. A storm had just rolled in, and rain doused the newly grown wildflowers. Maybe the wind disguised my footsteps, or perhaps Sverrir was just preoccupied with the battle. Either way, I heard his voice echoing from within one of the caverns. I ducked into a crevice and listened carefully, hoping he might let something slip—any insight into his strategy could help our side secure a victory."

I leaned forward, my meal long forgotten.

"But Sverrir wasn't talking strategy. Instead, he spoke of revenge. And the woman he conversed with didn't sound quite of this world. I later realized that he was channeling *her*."

"Her who?" Raynor asked.

"The woman Sverrir lost long ago," Torstein said. "The one whose death set him on his dark path. He promised to retrieve her from a dark world by opening a portal—many portals, if need be. *That* was why he wanted a crystal. *That* was the reason he'd started the mage war. It was all for her."

"Isn't it always? Ow!" Raynor rubbed his ribs and frowned at Brigga.

"Just listen," she hissed.

"We were completely isolated at the sea caves," Torstein continued. "I could have taken him out right then."

"Why didn't you?" Axel asked.

"I was afraid," Torstein admitted. "Sverrir was rumored to be the most powerful of his kind, and I was still a relatively young practitioner. I knew there was a chance he could kill me, and our numbers were already so low."

"What did you do?" Janna asked.

"I ran back to my camp. I collected three of our strongest mages and returned to the cave, only to find that he'd gone."

"No," I whispered.

"The final battle began shortly after that. Many mages were massacred. But only one crystal was imbued with the power of the alignment, and Ama and I fought Sverrir to claim it. As you know, we shattered it into a dozen pieces and divided them. I distributed half of the stones around the Northern Territories, while Ama hid the remaining six around this region—what's now Southern California. Sverrir followed her here. When he discovered she'd already hidden the crystals, he tried to torture their location from her. She refused and, well . . ."

My heart tugged. "I'm sorry, Torstein. She was a valiant warrior to protect her secret until the end."

"She was light incarnate." Moisture glistened in Torstein's eyes. "After I'd mourned her loss, I set out to avenge her death. Sverrir was a master at concealing his location, and though I was unable to kill him, I was able to discern the identity of the woman he'd spoken to in that cave. And learn the reason he was so determined to open a portal."

"How did you do that?" Janna asked. "I thought dark mages lived in obscurity."

"Most do." Torstein took a drink from his glass. "But Sverrir wasn't born into a family of mages. As I traveled up and down the coast, I determined that he'd come from a small fishing village at the southernmost tip of the Northern Territories. His clan was honorable—they took care of their land and helped any strangers who crossed their shores. The gods gifted their chieftain a special dagger—the crystals on its hilt were imbued with the gods' own magic, so that the dagger could manifest any object its wielder intended."

Holy Mother Frigga.

I reached under the table and dug my nails into Axel's thigh.

"Ouch," he muttered.

"We have a crystal-encrusted magical dagger," I whispered. "Do you think the gods created *two*?"

Axel arched one brow. "Or did ours have a previous owner?"

Can that even be possible?

"The chieftain used the dagger well," Torstein continued. "He called on its magic to build homes that withstood the harsh sea winds, to clothe wayward travelers who washed up on his shores, and during a particularly difficult winter, to save his people from the brink of starvation. He used his gift for the good of his community, and when he died, the relic was meant to pass on to his daughter—a young woman named Bodil, with whom Sverrir had fallen in love."

"Did it?" Janna asked, at the same time Raynor muttered, "Dark mages can love?"

"Everyone can love. *Raynor.*" Brigga delivered a swift elbow to his side.

"Sorry." He rubbed his arm.

Torstein leaned back. "Bodil took possession for only a week before the relic disappeared. A boy from a neighboring clan crept into the village under the cloak of night to steal the dagger. Of course, he didn't know how to wield it properly. He accidentally opened a portal to a dark realm, and a creature emerged. It took hold of the chieftain's daughter, drawing her into the darkness before the boy could close the portal. Sverrir flew into a rage—village legends recount that as the moment he turned dark. He murdered the boy and took the dagger for himself. He was adamant that no one should benefit from its magic until he could reopen the portal and retrieve his love. Of course, when the gods saw that their gift had fallen into unvirtuous hands, they promptly revoked it."

"They took the dagger back?" I blinked.

Torstein nodded. "There remains in that village a charred mark exactly where the dagger was last seen. A lightning bolt carried it from the village to the heavens. It has remained with the gods ever since."

"Or it got regifted to us," Axel muttered.

"I visited numerous villages," Torstein continued. "And over time, I learned that Sverrir spent the next several hundred years searching for the dagger—he never believed it was truly with the gods. While he searched, he studied dark magic and continued on his quest to reunite with his love. The only piece of his story I was unable to understand was Valkyris. In the cave he vowed to destroy your home. But to this day, I do not know how it connected to his pain."

Axel stared at me—the question in his eyes. Should we trust Torstein with our deepest secret? The one that had led us to hide our island for so long, and the exposure of which could very well result in our deaths? Odin only knew how many present-day humans would kill to own a magical dagger—the very one I now wore strapped to my back. But if we didn't tell Torstein . . . and if we didn't use every possible advantage to keep Sverrir from obtaining it . . .

I glanced at Janna. Her subtle nod confirmed the feeling in my gut.

"Do it, Axel." I squeezed his thigh. "He can help us."

Axel angled his head at Torstein. "You say Sverrir thought the dagger was still somewhere on earth? He spent centuries hunting for it?"

"Yes." Torstein glanced at the dimming sky. "Before the alignment and the creation of the crystal, he believed it was the only way to open the portal to retrieve his love."

"Well . . ." Axel drummed his fingertips on the table. "It would seem that we're in possession of *both* of his desired relics. You have half of the crystals. And we, uh . . . Ingrid?"

I reached behind my head, slid my fingers into the neck of my shirt, and withdrew the object sheathed at my spine. I set it on the table with a steadying breath. "We have the dagger."

"It can't be." Torstein exhaled heavily. "All accounts say the gods took it back."

"Apparently sometime after they did that, they gave it to us." I slid one finger along its blade. "Or to our chieftess, at any rate. We had no idea it had a previous owner."

"But how did it . . ." Torstein's eyes were wide. "Have you been carrying it with you all this time?"

I nodded.

"And you've not used it since you've came to Los Angeles?" Torstein asked.

"We don't really know how," Janna admitted. "We only have it because we needed it to jump times. Back home, our chieftess keeps it under lock and key. She and our chieftain used it to create a society based on fairness and valor and the greatest good for all. But Freia and Halvar's ideals are rare for our time—and ours is a clan that many want to overtake."

Torstein smiled sadly. "Selfishness permeates in this era as well."

"Wait." Brigga held up her hand. "If the mage war was six hundred years ago—"

"Give or take," Torstein said.

"Okay, so say it was *several* hundred years ago," Brigga corrected. "And our home exists roughly a thousand years ago. Then why is Sverrir so intent on destroying Valkyris in *our* time—before the mage war? Where—when—we live, he's aligning with powerful clans, and using his magic to bring us down. But Freia hasn't told anyone outside Valkyris that we have the dagger. Most of our residents don't even know about it!"

Axel rubbed lightly at his neck. "I'm guessing Sverrir attacked us for two reasons. One, he's a dark mage. And we're a clan intent on bringing good throughout the world. Those values are inherently at odds. And two, he's probably just taking wild stabs at where the dagger might be—going after every group with the kind of strength that might be gods-given."

"I suppose," Brigga said. "And *now* if he wipes Valkyris from existence—if we never exist—then the gods can't send their dagger to us. He may think that by taking us out, he'll have an easier time tracking his prize, and opening the portal, and saving . . ."

We all fell silent for a long moment.

"But he knows we have the dagger," Janna finally said. "He saw it on the night we arrived."

"And we'll continue to keep it from him," I said. "And your crystals too, Torstein. If he doesn't have what he needs to enact his spell, he can't control the realms—or make Valkyris disappear."

"He's not going to let up," Torstein warned. "He's spent a thousand years trying to reunite with his love."

"Then we're going to have to make sure that they *are* reunited," Axel said grimly. "In Helheim."

"Axel," I hissed.

"Look," Axel said. "I have no intention of dying anytime soon. And he clearly has no intention of letting us live. So the only thing we can do is connect him with his girlfriend. Either open the portal ourselves and send him packing, or kill him and trust the gods to send his spirit in the right direction. The one *way* south of Valhalla."

Janna apprised Axel. "Our orders were to bring him in. I'm not sure sending him through a portal would please Freia. What if he aligned with a giant and came back even more powerful than he already is?"

"So, Janna votes to kill him." Axel looked around. "Anyone else?"

"I didn't say—"

"We may not have a choice." I sighed. "If this is the mission he's been on for so long . . . do you really think there's any way we can ever be safe?"

"I think . . ." Janna stared at the ocean. "I think we'll face that fjord when we come to it. Right now, we have to find a way to capture him. He's wrought havoc in our era, and there's no telling how much he'll inflict in this one."

"We've been trying for weeks." Raynor groaned. "We're no closer than when we arrived. Even with our newly acquired light mage."

"That's it," Torstein whispered.

"What's it?" I asked.

"Now that I know how all of you fit into the picture, we may be able to bait him."

Axel growled. "I don't like where this is going."

"Neither do I." Torstein raised his palms. "And I don't want to put any of you at risk. But let me do more research into that Palos Verdes resonance. Tonight's conversation sparked an idea—one I want to examine before I assess its risk. If it's too great, I won't ask for your help. But if the risk can be managed, then there may be a chance we can entrap him once and for all."

"This plan better be good," Axel said.

"It will be," Torstein swore. "Gods willing."

For all of our sakes, I hoped he was right.

CHAPTER 20

"**A**ND THAT'S HOW MY** little sister taught *me* to roof jump. Isn't that wild?" A white-haired woman tossed her head back. A giggle pealed from her lips as she finished her tale.

It was the day of our alumni tea, and the Kappa Mu lawn was filled with linen-covered tables, current and past members, and the joyful sound of laughter.

"My *goodness*, Betsy. I cannot believe you did that!" The old lady to Betsy's left wiped a tear from her eye. "And to think, the housemother was *asleep* while you were hanging right outside her window."

"I very nearly got caught." Betsy picked up her teacup. "Can you *imagine*? It was eleven at night, for heaven's sake! A full two hours after curfew! Goodness, I miss living in this house."

"Would you like some more tea?" I stepped to Betsy's right and lifted the pot with a smile.

"Yes, thank you." Betsy leaned in slightly so I could

pour. "I'm sorry, darlin'—what did you say your name was?"

"Ingrid." I topped off her cup and filled her neighbor's.

"My Edwin has a sister named Ingrid." Betsy's eyes sparkled. "Of course, he was an Alpha—we met during rush week, and I was just absolutely smitten. Though I had to wait two whole years before he pinned me! It was the longest two years of my life."

"And now you've been married for fifty." Another elderly woman raised her teacup. "Here's to all of the friendships, marriages, children, and grandchildren we owe to Kappa Mu."

"Kappa Mu!" The women raised their cups in a celebratory toast.

Betsy pointed to an empty seat. "Why don't you join us, Ingrid? The party's nearly over. Surely you can take a break and tell us about what the house is like now. Do you still have study parties with the boys next door?"

"Or go dancing at the Roosevelt?" another woman chimed in.

"Bonfires at the beach?" asked a third.

"Bonfires are banned on public beaches." Betsy waved. "It's a fire hazard nowadays."

"Oh. Right."

"Actually, I should refill your scones." I picked up the empty plate. Lexi had been *very clear* that servers weren't to sit until the last guest had left. And I'd been trying to play nice ever since Monday night's showdown. "It looks like you preferred the strawberry and chocolate chip ones, *ja?*"

"The orange currant were good too," one of the women said hopefully.

"Done." I smiled as I carried my teapot back to the kitchen. Once there, I set it on the counter, filled a plate with the requested scones, and headed outside. I'd just reached the porch when Janna jogged up the steps.

"Someone's here to see us." She tilted her head toward a black vehicle parked on the street. Its driver climbed out of the car and stared at our table-covered lawn.

"Is that Torstein?" I squinted at the long-haired man lowering his sunglasses. "Why would he come to campus?"

"Not sure." Janna shifted her scone platter to one hand. "But I checked with Kayla, and she says since it's after three, we can go."

"Lexi was pretty clear that *nobody* was off duty until the last alumnae said goodbye."

"Lexi can stuff it."

I turned toward Brigga's voice. "Where'd you come from?"

"Table six." She pointed. "And if Kayla says we're done, we're done. Torstein's never showed up without warning. He must have gotten a read on one of the crystals."

"Or on our target." Janna narrowed her eyes. "I'll go see what he wants. You two finish with your tables and meet me upstairs in three. We'll have to figure out how to get our weapons past all of these civilians."

"We're in a theatre group, remember?" Brigga winked.

"Right . . ." I drew my shoulders back. "Okay. See you upstairs."

I quickly delivered the scones to my table, cleared the finished plates, and returned to the kitchen. After untying my apron and setting it on the counter, I spotted Brigga and Janna charging up the stairs. Whatever Torstein had told them, it must not have been good.

"Thanks, Carla," I called to our cook. She waved cheerfully from the end of the island countertop where she was elbow-deep in flour. "Do you mind if I grab a few scones to go? They smell amazing."

"Help yourself!" She tilted her head toward the wall. "Containers are in the pantry."

"Thanks." I quickly filled a small box and climbed the stairs. I wasn't sure what the rest of the afternoon would entail, but if we needed sustenance, I had us covered.

I hope.

Janna looked over as I jogged into our room. "Good. You're here. Suit up. Weapon up. Torstein got another crystal hit."

I closed the door behind me and traded my sundress for training gear. I slipped into my fitted black pants and sleeveless top, then cinched my weapons belt tight around my waist. "Where was it this time?"

"Palos Verdes again." Janna clipped her shield to her back. "I didn't ask for more details—he made it sound like time was of the essence."

"Then I guess we'd better move." I double-checked that Freia's dagger was secure on my back before popping my own shield into place. Then I slid my sword into its sheath and stuck an extra dagger to my calf. "I'm ready."

"Me too." Brigga marched to the door. "Any instructions?"

"Same as always." Janna palmed the hilt of her sword. "Don't die."

"That's good advice." Brigga opened the door and stepped onto the landing. Janna and I followed her out, and the three of us jogged down the stairs and to the porch. Torstein was already in the driver's seat, drumming his fingertips on the wheel.

"Better move," I whispered.

I marched determinedly across the lawn. As predicted, the remaining old women stared at us in surprise.

"Well, bless my soul. Are you putting on a play?" Betsy asked.

"Told you," Brigga muttered.

"Shakespeare in the Park rehearsal," I said. The cover had been gifted to us by a confused student the day we arrived. *Thank gods.* "It was great meeting you all. Betsy, stay off those roofs—you hear me?"

"I'll do no such thing!" Betsy laughed. "Have fun, girls!"

"Always do," I called back. I jogged the rest of the way to the vehicle where Axel and Raynor had already taken seats in the back. Torstein must have gone to get them while we'd been changing. I slid into the middle row and held my sword on my lap. "Okay, guru. What's the situation?"

Torstein turned his head. "Did you really just walk through a tea party dressed for battle?"

"Desperate times, Torstein." I narrowed my eyes. "Now fill us in on *everything* you know. We are *not* going to blow it this time."

By the time Torstein pulled up to the quiet forest on the bluffs of Palos Verdes, he'd fully briefed our team. Earlier that afternoon, the light mage was scanning for vibrations when he'd gotten another hit in the same location on the coast. The low, pulsing resonance matched the one emitted by his stones. This time around, he'd picked up a hint of darkness. It wasn't distinct enough to identify, but it definitely didn't fit with the peaceful, oceanfront community. When Torstein had directed his focus on the darkness, an intense heat shot back at him. And when he'd tried to zero in on it again, the heat—and the darkness—were gone.

He'd immediately jumped into his vehicle and shot along the freeway toward campus.

Our objectives were threefold. First, we hoped to recover one of the missing crystals. Any stone in our possession would be one less at Sverrir's disposal. Second, we wanted to locate the dark mage himself. Finding him would give us a shot at capturing him, which led us to our third goal. We hadn't decided whether this would be a kill mission, but capturing Sverrir was our endgame. Whatever happened after that, well . . .

Odin willing, we'd know what to do.

"Everybody know their places?" Janna climbed out of the car.

"Raynor and I will search the eastern side of the woods." Brigga stepped closer to her partner.

"Correct." Janna consulted the picture on Torstein's phone—a map of the woods surrounding something called the Wayfarers Chapel. "Axel, you and Ingrid will take the west side of the chapel. Go straight through the parking lot, and hang right just before you get to the glass church. And Torstein and I will cover the far side—it looks like it's the densest patch of forest, so if we need backup, we'll signal whoever's close. Remember, if anybody picks up on anything—anything at all— give three birdcalls and we'll meet up at the church. Got it?"

"Affirmative." Axel sheathed his sword. He withdrew an arrow and held it with his bow. "Sverrir's not escaping this time."

"He may not even be here," Torstein reminded us. "The darkness disappeared before I could confirm a presence. But I think the crystal *is*—or at least, it was. So let's get moving."

"Stay safe." I saluted my captain.

"You too," Janna responded.

With a nod, I turned on one heel and jogged for the trees.

"Wait up." Axel's footsteps fell softly behind me.

"No time." I spotted the chapel—a truly breath-taking wood and glass structure that was barely notice-able among the trees. "Whoa. This is gorgeous."

"How does it stand?" Axel matched my pace. "The supports are . . . huh. I guess I see how it works."

"Admire later, Andersson. Hunt now." I scanned from side to side as I ran, searching the forest for any sign of our dark mage. Or a crystal.

"See anything out of the ordinary?" Axel asked.

"No." I frowned. "But I'm not familiar with this region. For all I know, those weird trees over there are a portal to some unknown world where—hold on." I dug my boots into the ground. My heart pounded in my chest, its rhythm slowing as I drew a series of steadying breaths.

"What is it?" Axel raised his bow to eye level and turned in a slow circle.

"Do you feel that?" I asked.

"No. Just tell me where to shoot and I'll shoot."

"It's not a threat." I breathed deeper. "At least, I don't think it is. It's . . ."

"Talk, Ingrid," Axel growled.

"I feel . . . still. Peaceful." I met Axel's eyes. "It's the same way I felt when Torstein showed me his crystals."

"*Showed you his crystals?*" Axel shook his head. "I won't ask. Just tell me what you need."

"Cover me while I follow this . . . feeling." I shook my head. My tracking abilities had always relied on empirical evidence—footprints, soil samples, scraps of fabric torn off by a branch. I'd never *felt* my way toward anything before. Then again, I'd never looked for a magic rock before. Or traveled a thousand years into the future. Or had to assimilate to life in a twenty-first century sorority house.

It had been a month of firsts.

"This way." I followed the overwhelming sense of calm to my left. Something nudged at my back. I turned, drawing my fighting dagger.

"You hear something?" Axel asked from fifteen feet behind me.

"Did you just tap me?"

"No." Axel swung his bow in my direction. "Do you think someone's cloaked?"

"There it is again." I spun around, but nobody was there. "My gods, I think I'm going crazy."

"Check Freia's dagger. Make sure it's still secure." Axel kept his bow drawn while I reached behind my back. When my fingertips pressed against the hilt, a pulse shot up my arm. It was warm, and slow, and felt like liquid peace.

Liquid peace? Gods, you've been hanging out with Kenzi for too long.

"Dagger's secure," I confirmed. "But it's giving off this weird . . ."

Recognition slammed into me.

"Oh. My. Gods." I exhaled.

"What?"

"Freia's dagger . . . the stones . . . this . . . this *feeling*."

"Start making sense, Shieldmaiden, or I'm throwing you over my shoulder and getting you and that dagger as far away from here as possible."

"It's not *someone* that's tapping at my back. It's *something!*"

"Not better," Axel said.

"Freia's dagger is connected to the crystals! It's pushing me in the direction it wants to go!"

Axel's eyes narrowed. "You sure about that?"

"Absolutely," I said. "Watch."

I took four steps toward Axel. As I lifted my foot again, there was a tug at my back.

"See?" I said.

"No." Axel frowned. "Are you positive you're okay?"

"Just follow me. I know where we're going. Or, Freia's dagger does."

"Okay," Axel said. "But stay quiet. And keep your blade ready. Odin only knows what we're walking into."

I raised my fighting dagger and turned around. I walked silently across the dirt, avoiding errant branches until a pressure built below my left shoulder.

"Left up here," I whispered.

I swung one leg then the other over a toppled tree. Leaves crunched beneath my feet as I landed stealthily. I ran a quick scan to make sure we weren't being followed. The road was a good two hundred meters behind us, and the chapel was at least a two minute run away. Thick trees shielded us on one side, while a series of ferns dotted the sparser landscape to the other. I didn't see any movement, save for the occasional bird flitting overhead. And I hadn't spotted anything that didn't clearly belong to deer, squirrels, or mice. As far as I could sense, we were completely alone in this section of the forest.

So why do I feel so weird?

"Everything all right?" Axel cleared the log.

"I don't see any threats. But something feels off."

"Mmm." Axel turned a tight circle. "You want to turn back?"

"Have I *ever* quit on a mission?"

Axel took a step closer. "I've got you covered. Just track the crystal and let's get the Helheim out of here."

"Sounds good." I pushed my unease aside and followed the nudges at my back.

Left at a redwood. Right at a fallen log. Another two lefts near mossy boulders.

By the time I reached an arbor of white-barked trees, the nudges at my back finally stopped. An instinct I didn't recognize sent me to my knees, and I dug my fingers into the soft dirt. "I think it's here," I whispered. "Either that or I'm slightly crazy."

"I already knew that about you." Axel spoke without a hint of irony.

"Hey!"

"Crazy gets the job done." He kept his arrow at eye-level. "You think normal people would sign up for our jobs?"

My fingertips stung as I unearthed a rock. "I think I need an actual tool."

"Doubt there are any shovels out here. What about . . ." Axel looked left, then right. "Ah. Hold on." He jogged to a nearby tree and returned with a thick piece of bark. "You want me to dig or keep watch?"

"You keep watch. Your aim's better than mine."

"So you're finally admitting it, huh?" Axel tossed me the improvised tool. "About time."

"Shut up, Axel."

"I'm just glad you can see these things as they are." Axel puffed out his chest. "But don't worry, I'm sure I can teach you my—"

"I said." I dug into the dirt with my bark-shovel. "Shut." *Dig.* "Up." *Dig. Dig.* "You're distracting me."

"What's the number one thing I drilled into you at the academy?"

I heaved another pile of dirt over my shoulder. "How completely arrogant and irritating you are?"

"Such distorted memories." Axel sighed. "I was going for *victors remain focused in even the most distracting of circumstances.* You think the enemy's not going to pull every advantage in battle? Think he'll stay quiet and follow the choreography you worked out in training?"

"I've been in battle, you idiot." I flung another shovel-full of dirt. Then another.

"Language, Ingrid." Axel tutted.

"Stop irritating me while I'm trying to—oh! I hit something!" I tossed the bark to the side and used my nails to dig around the cool, solid object wedged firmly beneath two feet of dirt. It was caked in mud and clearly unwilling to budge. With a grunt, I drove my dagger along its thickest side and wiggled it slightly loose. "Ugh." I fell back on my heels. "I can't get enough leverage. Got any water?"

Axel tossed me the flask from his belt. "Here."

"Thanks." I undid the lid and poured the liquid in a small circle around the object. Then I used the tip of my dagger to carve out a moat.

"That work?" Axel asked.

"I think so. Let me just . . ." I stabbed the earth, working my blade until the object shifted from its place. "There! Oh, gods. Stay back!"

Axel did the opposite as a dim, blue flash erupted from the mud. He stepped in and pulled me to my feet as a pulse of heat burst from the ground. The object glowed, its caked-on dirt cracking until a lightning-shaped fissure formed across its surface. Axel held tight to my bicep as the glow dimmed, then disappeared.

We blinked at the object now laying atop the earth.

"Do we touch it?" Axel asked. "Or . . ."

"I suggest we get it out of here." I freed my arm

from Axel's grip. "We're too exposed, and something still doesn't feel right."

"But is it a crystal?" Axel leaned over, his bow momentarily forgotten.

"Only one way to find out, I guess."

I picked up the flask and poured the remaining water on the object. My hands moved quickly to rub the mud free, and my pulse quickened as the white-blue surface became more visible.

"This is definitely what's in Torstein's hideout," I confirmed. "Signal the others, and we'll get this thing out of . . . oh, gods."

"Oh gods, what?" Axel's bow was at the ready again.

"Did you feel the ground shake?"

"No. But if you did, we'd better get—"

A sharp jolt launched me backward. I held tight to the crystal as I soared through the air, landing with a thud behind Axel. The earth rocked beneath my bottom, and I scrambled to stand. Either Southern California was having one of its earthquakes, or Axel and I had triggered some kind of an alarm. Maybe Torstein's girlfriend had set a protection around the crystal, and when we removed it we'd—

"Ingrid! Look out!" Axel dropped his bow and threw his body across mine. He wrapped his arms around me so I was shielded from the brunt of the impact as we rolled across the rocky dirt. We landed painfully against the base of a tree. Axel raised himself on his forearms and quickly assessed me for injuries. "You okay?"

"What's happening?" I squirmed out of his grasp and pushed myself to my feet.

"I'm pretty sure we're under attack. That boulder just landed where you were sitting." He jumped up and spun around. "The threat came from my twelve o'clock."

"Great." I used one hand to slip the crystal into the pouch at my waist. With the other, I sheathed my fighting dagger and swapped it for my sword. "Hurry up. We need to alert the rest of our team before there's another—"

"On it."

Axel cawed loudly before turning his arrow to the spot where we'd unearthed the stone. A small, black circle hovered in the air just above the dig site. Axel fired an arrow into the hole. It disappeared as if it had been sucked straight into a void.

"What the Helheim?" Axel fired again. The second arrow was absorbed into the darkness.

"I don't think that's working."

Axel swore as the hole doubled in size. Now a faint layer of red sparked at its edges.

This was definitely not good.

"Take the crystal and run," Axel instructed. "I'll make sure nothing follows you."

"I'm not leaving my teammate." I had to shout—wind now swirled around the hole. "If something crawls out of that thing, we're facing it together."

"What if it pulls us in?" Axel shouldered his bow and drew his sword. He dropped to a fighting stance as the hole doubled again. Then again. Heat shot from its edges, instantly spiking the temperature of the once-cool forest.

This is so not good.

"We're not getting pulled in." I hooked my elbow around a low-hanging branch and held tight. "Grab onto something!"

"Good call."

A fierce gust burst from the darkness. Its heat lapped at my face, and I ducked my head to lessen the burn.

Augh! That hurts!

I rolled my head to the side to find Axel gripping a nearby branch.

Our eyes locked in a silent stare-down. Axel would have my back, no matter what obstacles were thrown at us. Just as he'd had it from the first moment he'd arrived in Clan Bjorn. He may have been a massive pain, but he was also my teammate. My equal. The partner I wanted at my side in this battle, and every battle hereafter.

We squared our shoulders to the threat, and I took a deep breath.

Just as a fire monster clawed out of the hole.

CHAPTER 21

"WHAT THE HELHEIM IS that thing?" Axel shouted over the wind.

"Judging by the blaze ripping across its body, I'm going to go with *fire monster*!" I raised my sword, preparing for battle.

"It's fire *giant*. And I thought they were supposed to be bigger." Axel cocked his sword arm and dropped back in a lunge.

He had a point. The monster stood just four-feet tall, with bulbous features and spindly arms and legs. Fire lapped at its limbs, shooting upward in red and orange sparks. It moved with the grace of a wounded turtle, and for a moment I thought that it might not pose a real threat.

Then it scooped a fireball off of its leg and flung it straight at Axel.

"Look out!" I screamed as the fireball struck Axel's leg. Flames immediately encompassed his calf. He ripped off the branch he'd been holding and beat it against his leg. The fire dimmed, sparked, then went out.

Valkyrians, one. Fire monster, zero.

For now.

"We need to get it back in that portal," I yelled.

"Agreed. But he's never going to let us near it—or him. He'll keep firing—literally—until we're ash."

"We have to find a way around him." I quickly skimmed the forest. We'd be too exposed if we went left, but to the right stood several clusters of trees. They very nearly formed a wall. "What if we went that way?" I pointed. "We could hide behind those trees and could come out on the other side of the portal."

"Or he could catch us on the move and char us on the spot. The gaps are too big to shield fireballs. But . . ."

I followed his sight line. An intricate network of branches connected the trees roughly fifteen meters above the ground. With the thickening smoke, it would be harder for the monster to spot us up there.

Of course, it would also be hard to *not fall to our deaths.*

Gulp.

"I'll go high," I offered. "You can stay low. Keep it distracted while I get to safety. Then I can pull its attention and convince it I'm the bigger threat so it attacks me while you herd it toward the—"

"Ingrid! Duck!"

I flung myself to the ground as a second fireball

soared across the forest. This one arced directly over my body. It hit the tree behind me, cloaking its trunk in a blanket of flames. By the time I'd righted myself, the bottom half of the redwood was completely engulfed . . . and it had passed its condition along to two of its neighbors.

I pointed my sword at a cluster of trees roughly ten meters away. "I'll climb those and try to drive him backward."

"Good." Axel shuffled to the side, narrowly avoiding a third fireball. "I'll come around from his right. Be careful of the—"

He jumped again.

"Fire. Got it." With a nod, I shoved my sword into its sheath. Then I turned and raced for the cluster. The air was already thick with smoke, it's cloying grey tendrils snaking swiftly through the forest. I leapt over a mossy log, then pushed off a boulder and launched myself at a wide, brown trunk. My feet sought purchase on a knob, and I dug my fingertips into a dense brick of bark. It came free, dropping to the ground and shifting my balance just enough that I flailed. I jumped backward, landing lightly on my toes and pivoting as a series of fireballs flew at Axel. The assassin charged forward, dodging and weaving while holding the monster's attention with the fierce swinging of his sword. He was buying me time— distracting the demon so I could safely scale the trees. The only problem was, redwoods didn't have many low branches. And I hadn't thought to bring a rope.

Think, Ingrid. What would Janna do?

My captain and I had spent plenty of hours climbing the cliffs back home—she'd *definitely* have found a way to scale these red-barked behemoths. I quickly assessed my surroundings. None of the nearby trees had limbs low enough to climb. And none of the fallen boughs looked strong enough to use as a rope—if I grabbed one to circle a trunk and inch my way up, it would no doubt break. But the trees directly in front of me stood in a fairly tight cluster. Two looked sufficiently close for me to wedge between them and climb in a star formation. Assuming the bark didn't give out beneath my boots, I *might* just make it to the bottom limb. And if not, well . . .

I'd deal with that problem later.

A surge of heat erupted behind me, and I glanced over my shoulder to find Axel dodging a massive blast. The fire monster now shot streams from his hands. One struck the ground directly to my boyfriend's right. Axel spun to the left, raising his sword as he drew the monster's attention toward the ocean side of the forest. I'd have to move fast—at this rate, the entire area would be on fire before I made it halfway up this tree. With a steadying breath, I wedged my palms against the two trees, dug my toes into opposite trunks, and climbed.

And climbed.

And climbed.

I knew better than to look down. Any distraction could cost me my position, and a lot was riding on my doing my job *exactly right*. But when Axel let out a cry, I couldn't help but turn my head. In the second it took me to realize he'd been hit by another fireball, my balance shifted backward. My hand slipped, and I dug my toes into the trunk to try to steady myself. But it was no use—I was going down. I arched my spine and pressed my feet even harder into the tree. The action reset my balance . . . but it also broke loose a thick chunk of bark, making my feet chatter lower.

Oh, gods.

I was easily fifty feet high. A fall from this elevation was simply not an option. So, I did the only thing I could think of. Bracing myself with my feet, I released my hold on the tree and ripped my fighting dagger from its sheath. I drove it into the tree and held tight. Then, I used the hilt to pull myself higher. The tool was just what I needed to wedge my feet into sturdier sections of bark. In my relief, I glanced down . . . and realized Axel was operating purely on the defensive. The monster continued to assault him with fireballs. And the rest of our team was still nowhere to be seen.

Climb, Ingrid.

With my footing once again secure, I withdrew the dagger before piercing the trunk a few feet higher. I pulled myself toward it, my feet inching slowly upward as I scaled to the nearest limb. It felt like an eternity before my hands wrapped around the thick branch, but as I carefully climbed atop it, I exhaled in relief. I'd made it.

Now to herd a fire monster.

I cupped my hands to my mouth and cawed. Axel stopped dodging fireballs long enough to point two fingers toward the portal.

"Got it," I shouted.

Axel shot me a thumbs-up just as the monster launched another stream his way. He somersaulted across the forest floor before jumping to his feet and charging toward the base of my tree.

"Do you see what he has on his neck?" Axel shouted.

I squinted through the smoke. "Is that . . ."

"Another crystal," he confirmed. "He's probably here to bring it to Sverrir. Don't herd him through the portal before I can cut it off."

"You can do that?" I yelled.

"There's very little I *can't* do." He smirked. "Thought you knew that by now."

Oh, the ego. But because I couldn't help myself, I called down, "Be safe."

"Back at you."

"Now get away from my tree before he burns it down."

Axel saluted, then charged in the opposite direction. With the monster's attention diverted, I scanned the row of trees between me and the portal. There were no more than a dozen, and since this part of the forest was mostly clusters, I had a fairly straightforward path to my goal. All I had to do was climb from one limb to the next—without falling, and without getting incinerated. So long as I didn't look down things should be fine. *Right?*

Don't think. Just move.

On it.

I focused on the neighboring branch, gripped my dagger in one hand, and carefully climbed to my feet. I stretched my arms out, testing my balance and angling my blade downward so I'd be ready to stab the tree if things went south.

Then I jumped.

Panic seized my chest as I soared through the air. It wasn't far—maybe eight feet. But I was fairly sure my heart stopped beating before my feet landed on the nearby limb. My torso tipped forward, and I stepped quickly to hug the trunk before permitting myself a slow exhale of relief.

One tree down. Eleven more to go.

The next series of jumps were decidedly less terrifying. Once I'd taken *one* death-defying leap, the rest came fairly easily. I'd just begun to relax the grip I held on my dagger when a loud *whoosh* sounded from below. It was promptly followed by an agonized cry.

"Axel! No!"

Time froze as I clung to my branch. Axel stood in a small clearing, his spine arched and his hands tearing at his shirt. Flames lapped at his back as the fire monster shot a ceaseless stream from its mouth. Red and orange bursts sparked along Axel's torso, swirling upward until they'd turned him into a human candle.

"Roll on the ground!" I screamed, but a crack of fire overpowered my voice. "Axel!"

"I have him." The words came on a furious roar.

Torstein emerged from the ferns, covered in dirt and pulsing with anger. In the seconds it took him to run across the forest, the smoke cleared and the temperature dropped. His powers clearly outranked the fire breather's. For a second, it seemed as if we might just get this under control.

That was when the monster attacked.

CHAPTER 22

T HE FIRE MONSTER DROPPED to his knuckles and ran for Axel on all fours. His animalistic howl morphed into a hiss as he opened his mouth and spewed fire. The stream hit Axel square on, forcing him to the ground and engulfing his body in a raging inferno while I clung helplessly to a tree.

"Do something!" I screamed at Torstein.

The light mage had already raised his arms. As the monster knuckled forward, Torstein stood perfectly still. He closed his eyes and shot a white beam from his palms. It swirled around Axel, cloaking him in a thick, azure mist that instantly doused the flames. *Thank gods.*

Torstein angled his hands toward the fire monster and shot again. The beast howled with rage as the magical mist wrapped around him. His flames disappeared, leaving black wisps of smoke streaming from what looked to be a disturbingly muscular body. The creature was clearly more animal than human. And if the glint in its steely, red eyes was any indication, Torstein had just triggered its fight reflex in a whole new way.

Get up, Axel!

"What's happening?" Axel shouted. "I can't see!"

"Don't move—I'm healing you," Torstein yelled back. "You'll be clear in half a minute."

"And I'll cover you until then."

Oh, thank gods! Janna's voice filled me with relief. If she was on the ground, the fire monster didn't stand a chance.

"Torstein, hold that thing off until Axel's back in commission." Janna positioned herself between the assassin and the monster. "If you slip, I'm here as backup."

"I never slip," Torstein said easily.

The fire monster hissed. Torstein doused it in another white wave. The creature stamped its feet to the ground, and Janna shifted just enough to shield Axel while he stood.

"Holy Helheim." Axel blinked at his recently-charred arm. "It doesn't even hurt."

"Then help me kill this thing," Janna ordered.

"Wait!" Axel leaned closer to Janna. He must have whispered our plan, because Janna shifted her attention to the trees and gave me a nod. Then she raised her shield to her chest and charged.

The monster tensed its back. A row of flames erupted from its spine. Torstein promptly doused them with a beam, earning a hearty howl from the creature.

Axel and Janna drew close enough to strike. Each slashed violently at their opponent while he whipped his head from side to side—he was probably looking for a weakness. My teammates tried to push him back —to get him near the portal that still swirled just a few leaps away from my current position. With no time to lose, I jumped to the next tree. And then the next. And the next. With the portal finally behind me, I carefully turned on my branch and traded my dagger for my sword.

This better work.

"Hey!" I waved my sword back and forth, hoping the fire on the ground would reflect in its blades. Janna and Axel had succeeded in driving the monster so it should have been able to hear my shout. If I could only convince it that *I* was the danger it needed to pursue . . .

"Ingrid!" Axel shouted. "I don't have the crystal yet."

"Then hurry the Helheim up!" I waved my sword again. "Hey! You! Come and get me!"

The monster turned its head, likely assessing its new threat. As its eyes locked in on me, Axel lunged forward. He brought his sword down on the creature's neck, and it let loose with a wretched howl. Red seeped across the forest floor, but its head remained attached. If Axel had been trying to decapitate it, he'd need to use more—

"There it is!" Axel swiped his hand along the ground. He raised a triumphant fist, holding tight to the chained crystal. Objective completed!

Now to send the demon packing.

"It's all you, Shieldmaiden!" Axel called.

"Heeeeeyyyyy!" I shrieked from my treetop perch. When the fire monster looked up, I ripped a branch from the redwood and launched it at him. He hissed. I adjusted my sword so it caught the reflection of a nearby flame. The creature stamped his feet and took a step in my direction.

"That's it." I waved my blade so the flame appeared to move up and down. Hopefully, he thought I was a rival fire monster . . . or at least, a more immediate threat than Janna and Axel. We needed *any reason* for him to come just a little closer. Because if he did . . .

I ripped another branch and flung it into the closest fire. The flames eagerly consumed the fuel, surging upward in a burst of red, orange, and blue.

The fire monster lowered his head, dropped to his knuckles, and charged at my tree.

"Axel!" I yelled.

"On it!" He raced forward, coming alongside the fire monster and ramming into him with one shoulder. The creature stumbled. Axel's blow had shifted his trajectory enough to align him slightly more with the portal. But he was still off track.

"Again!" I screamed, twisting my sword so the flames reflected directly at the monster. Axel rammed him a second time. The creature stumbled over his knuckles, opening his mouth and shooting a burst at the assassin. Axel dropped and rolled, extinguishing his flaming shirt. The moment he went down, Janna raced in to take his place. She raised her shield and leapt at the fire monster. Her blow pushed the creature into a fallen log. He tripped on the wood, his muscular limbs flailing as he launched forward—toward the sparking portal. He tumbled across the dirt, stopping just shy of the goal. If Janna and Axel didn't push him through soon—

Whoosh!

A cool wind whipped across the forest. I clung to my tree as the breeze swept along the earth. A tornado of dirt swirled around the fire monster, lifting him toward the portal. Axel let out a battle cry as he leapt from the ground—shirt still smoking—and launched himself at his target. The monster yowled as Axel's shoulder struck his back. The next moment, the creature hurtled into the portal and back to whatever dark realm it had come from.

"Axel, fall back!" I screamed as the assassin stumbled forward. He was too close to the hole! If he got sucked in . . .

Axel swore as a cyclone tugged him upward. The wind circled around him, pulling him away just as the portal sparked, flamed, and snapped shut. The cyclone promptly dissipated, dropping Axel to the ground in an unceremonious heap.

"Ugh." Axel rolled to his side. "That hurt."

"Sorry." Torstein marched carefully across the forest, extinguishing fires with his hand-mist as he walked. "The wind thing is fairly new for me—I don't completely have it under control yet."

"The wind was you?" Janna called over her shoulder. She bent to offer Axel an arm and carefully helped him up. "You okay?"

"I've been better," he admitted. "I've also been worse, so I'm calling this a win. Ingrid? Are you all right?"

"Physically, yes. But I'm not sure how to get down from this tree." I stared at the limbless trunk stretching below me. "I didn't really think that far ahead."

"I can help with that." Torstein halted his mist stream and flicked his fingers upward. Another cyclone swept across the forest, climbing my tree trunk and whirling just beyond my reach. "Jump into it, Ingrid."

"No, thank you."

"Trust me."

"I thought you said you were new at wind." I was not about to put my life in the hands of an amateur weather wizard.

"Funnels are pretty basic. But if you'd prefer, you can try to climb down. I doubt you'll make it very far . . ."

"Ugh. Fine." I held tight to my sword, closed my eyes, and leapt to what I very much hoped was not my death. My hair whipped my face as I entered the cyclone, and I tried not to scream as I was lowered slowly to the ground.

What the Helheim had become of my life?

"Uff!" I groaned as my bottom slammed into the dirt.

"Sorry," Torstein called. "I'm still working on the touchdowns."

"Basic level my left arm," I grumbled. But I offered a sincere, "Thanks, Torstein," as I climbed shakily to my feet.

"*Ja*. Thanks, man," Axel said. "If you hadn't been here, I would have been incinerated."

"It was nothing." Torstein scanned the forest. "Though I am concerned for your friends. I didn't see Raynor or Brigga on my way to this side of the forest."

"Gods, I hope they're not—"

"What the Helheim happened here?" Brigga's panicked squeak echoed across the trees. She and Raynor appeared on the opposite side of the ferns. Dirt covered their faces, and their clothes were caked in mud.

"What the Helheim happened *to you*?" Axel asked.

"We came when we heard the signal—or, we tried to." Brigga crossed her arms. "But *somebody* got into it with a bobcat."

"What?" I blurted. "Are you hurt?"

"I'm fine." Brigga shook her head. "Raynor, however, may need stitches."

"It's not that bad." Raynor held tight to his forearm. "If I don't look at it."

"Bring it here." Torstein held up a hand. "I'm on healing duty today."

Raynor limped slowly across the ferns.

"How did you . . ." Axel shook his head. "Never mind. I don't want to know."

"It turns out there's a den not far from here," Brigga explained. "When we were searching the area, we came across some cubs and, well . . ."

"At least you're both okay. We all are." Janna nodded at Axel. "Right?"

Axel caught my eye. "Ingrid?"

"I'm good."

The assassin shook his head. "Today would have been a Hel of a lot easier if I'd had a dragon."

"You have dragons where you're from?" Torstein's brows shot up. "How do you utilize them?"

"Battle transport. Air assault." Axel shrugged. "The usual ways."

"I didn't realize you could . . . interesting. You know, if I had access to a moderate-sized lizard, maybe I could . . . ah. There you are." Torstein turned his attention to Raynor, who'd finally cleared the ferns. "Hold out your arm, and *do not move.*"

"What are you going to—ouch!"

"I said stay still." Torstein shook his head. Then he took Raynor's hand in his and set to work.

"You have a moderate-sized lizard at your house," I said to Axel. "Wonder what Rufus is up to right now."

"Not staving off fire monsters, that's for sure." Axel chuckled. He climbed carefully over a fallen log and crossed the forest until he stood directly in front of me. "Good job up there, Shieldmaiden. Way to get the job done."

"You too." I unclipped my shield from my back and let it fall to the ground. Then I ran my fingertips along

Axel's seemingly uninjured arms. "If I hadn't watched it, I'd never have known you got burned."

"Several times." Axel shook his head. "That thing was no joke."

"Seriously." I stared at the unblemished skin. "Guess it's good to have a light mage on our side."

"You're welcome," Torstein called. "There. Raynor, you should be all set. By the way, I'm assuming we have possession of the crystal we came to find?"

"We're in possession of *two*." Axel dug out the crystal he'd confiscated from the pouch at his waist, and I did the same.

"Two!" Torstein's eyes grew wide.

"The fire monster had one," I said. "But there was also one buried in the ground—just like you'd thought there would be."

"The fire monster had one?" Torstein shook his head. "Could that mean . . ."

Janna sheathed her sword. "You said that in the war, the dark mages wanted to use whole crystals to open portals to other realms. Do you think they're able to do that with just a fraction of one?"

"Gods, I hope not." I shuddered.

"Because that would mean that if they had possession of all twelve pieces . . ." Axel's eyes met mine.

"Odin only knows what they could unleash." I rested my forehead against Axel's chest.

A heavy silence blanketed the forest as I processed what we were up against. This was more than a disgruntled mage Hel bent on destroying our world—

which, in and of itself, was frightening enough. Now we could be facing the monsters of Muspelheim, Helheim, Svartalfheim . . . places I'd only heard of in stories, and that some part of me had always thought were purely imaginary. But what I'd seen today proved otherwise. And wistful thinking rarely won wars.

One day at a time, Ingrid.

Axel rubbed his hand along my back. "We'll take them down," he said easily. "We've never faced anything we couldn't handle before."

"True." I drew a breath. "And our team may not have dragons, but we do have Torstein. That has to count for something, right?"

"Ah. That's what I forgot." Torstein raised one finger. "Everyone sit tight. I'll be right back."

"Where are you go—oh!" I jumped as Torstein twirled his hand and a white oval appeared in front of him. He stepped casually through it and promptly disappeared. The oval closed with a crisp *snap*.

"Did he just leave us here?" Raynor asked.

"Yes," Brigga confirmed. "But he said he'd be back."

"And you believe him?"

"He did just help us banish a fire monster. Besides, I'm too exhausted to worry." Janna dropped beside a nearby log and rested her back against the bark. "Wake me when he comes back."

"Will do." Axel chuckled. "Ingrid and I are going to take a walk."

"We are?" I looked at him.

"Just a short one," he promised. "I think we're all pretty low on energy."

Truth.

I re-clipped my shield to my back and let Axel lead me away from our friends. We walked in silence, stepping over boulders and branches until we reached a garden of roses. A handful of white blooms peppered the low bushes, their presence this late in the season a tribute to either the mild climate or a near-magical caretaker. Maybe Torstein wasn't the only light mage in Los Angeles.

Could that possibly be . . . *no.*

Axel slipped his fingers through mine and pulled me forward. We walked until we came to the tall, wood and glass structure that very nearly blended in with the forest. Axel led me inside the chapel. He turned to face me, a look of pure vulnerability coating his normally stoic features. Then he swept me into his arms for a heart-stopping, mind-blowing, absolutely unforgettable kiss.

CHAPTER 23

W HEN AXEL AND I finally came up for air, the trees above the chapel's glass ceiling were no longer dappled with sunlight. We'd barely had a second alone since we'd gotten together, and the weeks of waiting combined with the relief at not being incinerated by a fire monster made this moment *extremely* pressing. But even though we'd banished the fire monster, it wasn't smart to leave our friends exposed in a possibly compromised forest.

No matter how good of a kisser Axel was.

"We should . . . probably . . . get back," I panted. "We'll want to get out of here before nightfall, and we're cutting it pretty close."

"Torstein's our ride." Axel's lips brushed against my ear. "And he left. So . . ."

Axel nipped lightly at the side of my neck. It took every ounce of restraint I possessed to place my hands on his chest and push him away.

"He said he'd be right back," I reminded him. "And technically, we're on a mission."

A low rumble vibrated from Axel's chest. "You're right. But we're going to have to find time to be alone at some point."

"Agreed." I sighed. "Just tell me that someday soon we'll be home in Valkyris, and everything will be back to normal."

"We will," Axel vowed. "And it will. But until then, please promise me you'll be safe. There was a minute back there when I thought you were going to fall out of that tree."

"That scared me too," I admitted.

"Good. Because it *terrified* me." He rested his forehead against mine. "Ingrid, I don't know what I'd do if anything ever happened to you. You have my heart. You know that?"

Heat flooded my cheeks. "I . . . uh . . . I—"

Axel stopped my stammering with a kiss.

"Just take care of my girl," he murmured as he pulled back. "Okay?"

A ridiculous grin spread across my face. *He said* my girl . . .

"Come on, Shieldmaiden." Axel slipped his fingers through mine. "Duty calls."

"Doesn't it always?" I let him lead me out of the chapel and through the dimming forest. We'd nearly reached the spot where we'd left our team when a burst of fire shot through the trees.

Axel swore loudly. "Did the monster come back?"

I pulled my shield from my back and unsheathed my sword. "Only one way to find out."

We raced through the forest, leaping over logs and ferns until we reached the clearing. I didn't see any portals—in fact, everything seemed to be in order. My friends stood calmly chatting to a cheerful Torstein. The light mage was focused on a massive, winged lizard snorting smoke from its nose.

Wait. What?

My heels dug into the dirt. "Is that—"

"A dragon?" Axel nearly dropped his sword. "Whose dragon is that?"

"It's yours." Torstein turned around with a smile.

"This isn't one of mine." Axel shook his head. "I know all the Valkyris dragons, and I don't recognize this one."

"That's because this isn't a Valkyris dragon. He's a California dragon. By way of your fraternity, actually." Torstein patted the animal's neck. "You said you had a mid-sized lizard in your room, so I ported in and grabbed this guy. I just finished transmuting him."

My jaw unhinged. That massive green beast was . . . *Rufus?*

"You turned my *iguana* into a *dragon?*" Axel tilted his head. "Are you mad? I don't have a barn. Where am I going to keep him?"

"In your room, of course." Torstein pointed to Rufus' leg. A thick, green bracelet circled the creature's

223

ankle. Torstein held out a black, human-sized one to Axel. "Take this and wear it at all times. I've enchanted the bands so they'll respond to your commands. You can order the dragon to come, go, shrink, or enlarge— just talk into the little speaker right here."

Torstein tapped the top of Axel's bracelet before depositing it in his palm.

"Are you serious?"

"You said a dragon would be useful," Torstein said. "And we're going to need every conceivable advantage in the days ahead."

"You made me a dragon." Axel shook his head. He slipped the communicator on his wrist and walked slowly toward Rufus. His eyes sparkled with pure joy. This was the best gift Torstein could possibly have given him.

"Thank you," I said to the light mage. "This means everything."

"*Ja.* Thanks, man." Axel didn't take his eyes off of Rufus. "I've really missed these guys."

"If I'd known we had a dragon rider, I might not have been so worried about our chances." Torstein looked at each of us in turn. "A dragon rider, two shieldmaidens, a warrior, and a wisdom bearer."

"Throw in a light mage, and you've got a pretty solid team, *ja*?" Janna kept her voice calm. But I knew her well enough to know that she was worried. We were facing an enemy who, apparently, had a previously unknown legion of dark monsters on his side. Janna had every right to be concerned.

We all do.

"Speaking of teams." Torstein folded his hands together. "Axel—do you remember the day we met? When I told you that you seemed familiar?"

"Sure." Axel slowly stroked Rufus' side. The iguana-dragon lowered his head to sniff his handler's arm. "*Hei*, boy. You're going to love flying."

"Well, I realized where I know you from. Or not *where*, rather, but *when*."

Torstein's words caught my attention. "What do you mean, *when*?"

"You're not from Valkyris," Raynor asserted. "And none of our warriors have encountered a light mage of your abilities. Not in our era, at any rate."

"No." Torstein spoke carefully. "But when I was young, I was a lot like your colony—I kept myself hidden, fearing my gift would make me a target. I spent many years alone on an island off the coast of the Northern Territories. It was there that I met two warriors from a land I'd never heard of—Valkyris."

Brigga let out a soft gasp. "You knew about us? In our time, I mean?"

"Not exactly," Torstein said. "I'd never encountered anyone from your clan, until the day I met Sigrid and Leif.

Axel's hand fell from Rufus' cheek. "What did you say?"

"Their boat washed up on my island. It was badly damaged—far beyond the point of repair. They'd been at sea for weeks, and they'd eaten through all of their rations. They were starving; exhausted; weak to the point of near death. I was too inexperienced in my practice to do more than a basic healing. But I'd built a sturdy home a safe distance from the shore, and my island had good soil for farming. I told them they could take my spot—that I'd find another place to live. They were desperate to get back home and offered to take me with them if they could procure another ship. I was afraid it was a trap—so many in that time feared magic-wielders, and my magic was still too new to me to control. I knew they'd be safe on my island, and so I fled. I tied together the few boards I could salvage from their boat and floated to another island. Then another. When I found one with good soil and a pond for drinking water, I built myself a new shelter. Centuries passed while I practiced my magic. When I was skilled enough to defend myself, I finally conjured a vessel and ventured into the greater world." Torstein apprised Axel. "I didn't think of that couple again until the night I met you. Something in your eyes reminded me of the man's . . ."

Where was he going with this?

"What did you say their names were?" Axel choked out the words.

"Sigrid and Leif."

Axel's hands trembled.

"Are you okay?" I inched closer and slowly slipped my fingers through his.

"And you said they were alive when you left them?" Axel didn't take his eyes off Torstein.

"Yes. They were recovering from their injuries, but they were very much alive."

Raynor stepped forward. "What year would you guess that was?"

"Near the end of the eleventh century? Beginning of the twelfth?"

Raynor exhaled sharply. He stared at Axel, who didn't appear to be breathing.

"Why?" Torstein asked. "Do you know the people I gifted my island?"

"I do." Axel's hand tightened around mine. "I think they were my parents."

What?

Axel's expression equal parts exhilarated and terrified. "And if you're right about the timeline . . . no. I can't . . ."

He swayed.

"What is it?" I asked gently.

Axel steadied himself as he met my gaze. "If he's right about the timeline, then where we're from—or, *when* we're from—my parents are still alive."

My mouth formed a small *O.* "Are you sure?"

"No," Axel admitted. "Torstein, you say that island could sustain life?"

"It had plenty of fish and good soil," Torstein confirmed. "It was my safe harbor for many years."

"But they would have tried to come home," Raynor countered. "They'd have built a boat and sailed for Valkyris. You said they were desperate to get back."

"That's true," Torstein said. "But the island had very

few trees. Unless another boat washed ashore, I'm afraid they were well and truly marooned."

"Poor things," Brigga whispered.

"I am incredibly sorry I took their boards. If I hadn't let my fear overtake me . . ." Torstein bowed his head. "Forgive me, Axel."

"What's done is done," Axel said quietly.

"Do you realize what this means?" I squeezed Axel's hand. "Torstein can tell us where the island is. When we get home, we can rescue your parents!"

Axel swayed again. This time it was Rufus who leaned closer, steadying the assassin.

"Snort." The iguana-dragon exhaled a puff of smoke.

Axel shook his head before looking at me. "Guess we've got one more thing to fight for, huh?"

I held his gaze. "I guess we do."

Janna stepped closer, keeping one eye on the still-snorting Rufus. "We're in this together, Axel. Always have been. Always will be."

"We'll find a way back to your parents," Brigga said. "I know we will."

"And we'll bring them home," Raynor vowed.

"I'll do everything in my power to help you," Torstein promised. "I owe you that . . . and more."

"Thanks," Axel said softly. "You all make one Hel of a team. You know that?"

I looked at my friends—my fierce captain, our light mage, the warrior, the disseminator, and the assassin who'd captured my heart. We were more than a team. We were a family—one I'd stumbled into on the most unlikely of journeys, and the one I'd give my life to protect . . . in this era and any other.

As the moon rose over the forest, I held tight to Axel's hand, took a deep breath, and issued our battle cry.

"Let's go save our worlds."

The Shieldmaiden Squadron returns in
SILENT SHIELD

Shieldmaiden Ingrid Tirsdatter is in the final leg of her very first mission. After chasing a dark mage one thousand years into the future, she and her team have spent the past two months trying to stop him from doing the unthinkable—enacting a magical spell that's certain to destroy their world. But when a collection of crystals goes missing, it's clear their enemy is making his final play. And when Axel starts acting peculiar, Ingrid realizes that more than just their home is on the line. If she and her team can't stop the dark mage, her past—and her future—may disappear forever.

Meet the rest of the Valkyris crew in
VIKING ACADEMY

Erik held me until my shoulders stopped shaking—whether it was a minute or an hour, I couldn't tell. The only things I knew for sure were:

1. *I was trapped a thousand years in the past, with little hope of ever going home. And,*
2. *I was wrapped in the arms of the most absurdly gorgeous Viking to have ever walked the face of the Earth.*

Maybe my old life was overrated.

When seventeen-year-old Saga Skånstad discovers an antique dagger, she's instantly sucked into a world where Vikings rule the seas and dragons roam the skies, and the only thing more dangerous than the chief who takes her captive is the rival who steals her away. The heir of Norway's most feared tribe is fierce, cold, and absolutely unyielding. With intruders encroaching upon his borders, Erik Halvarsson has little patience for the girl whose ignorance threatens his very existence. He enlists Saga in the magical Valkyris Academy, where she learns the skills she'll need to protect herself from foreign raiders and domestic terrors. But nothing can protect her from falling for the one guy in all the world she's absolutely forbidden to choose . . . or from risking everything to unlock the secrets that haunt him.

When darkness threatens Saga's new home, she must decide whether to return to the life she's always known, or fight for a love she never could have imagined. Her decision will determine a legacy—not only for Saga, but for the world she never knew she was fated to lead.

ACKNOWLEDGMENTS

To my amazing little family—thank you for always making me smile. I'm so grateful that God gave me you. To Lauren Clarke and her team at CREATING ink, who never fail to make our Norse crews shine. To Mariana, for keeping the Viking ship afloat. And to the readers who take these crazy voyages with me—thank you for believing in fairy tales.

And to MorMorMa. Always.

ABOUT THE AUTHOR

Before finding domestic bliss in suburbia, S.T. Bende lived in Manhattan Beach (where she became overly fond of Peet's Coffee) and studied Shakespeare in Europe... where she became overly fond of McVitie's cookies.

S.T.'s love of Scandinavian culture, and a very patient Norwegian teacher, inspired her YA Norse fantasy series'. And her deep love of a galaxy far, far away led to her writing children's books for the Star Wars franchise. As an experienced IP writer, she's written multiple books published by Disney-Lucasfilm Press and its licensees.

When she's not creating stories, S.T. dreams of skiing on Jotunheim and Hoth.

Learn more about the world of S.T. Bende at
www.stbende.com .